DISASTER AT THE CHRISTMAS DINNER

A Churchill & Pemberley Mystery Book 8

EMILY ORGAN

Disaster at the Christmas Dinner

Emily Organ

Chapter 1

"WHAT TIME DID THIS HAPPEN?" asked Annabel Churchill, transfixed by the prostrate body in the snow.

Mr Pouch scratched his grey beard. He was a lean and stooped man with large blue eyes. "Sometime in the night."

"Can you be any more specific?"

"We went to bed at ten o'clock and all was well. Then I looked out of the kitchen window at first light and saw him on the ground."

"Awful," said Doris Pemberley.

Churchill struggled to muster the courage required for her next question, the brutality was difficult to bear. "Where's his head?"

"I found it in pieces over there." Mr Pouch pointed at the tree in the centre of the garden. "I followed the footprints over to the oak. I think the head was thrown against the trunk."

Churchill winced.

"How could anyone be so cruel?" whimpered Pemberley.

"Let me show you what's left of the head." Mr Pouch led them over to the tree and stooped to pick something up off the ground. "The nose was snapped in half." He held up a piece of carrot for them to inspect.

"What about his eyes?" asked Churchill.

"I used two small pieces of coal. Not very original, I know. They'll be around here somewhere." He looked about on the ground. "Oh, there's one by your foot, Miss Pemberley."

Pemberley grimaced and shrank away from it.

Large, fat snowflakes floated down from the leaden sky. Churchill pulled her woolly hat over her ears and surveyed the scene. "We need to establish whether this barbaric act was aimed at the snowman or yourself, Mr Pouch," she said. "Have you upset anyone recently?"

His jaw dropped. "Upset anyone? I've never upset anyone in my entire life."

Although Churchill considered this unlikely, Mr Pouch did strike her as a fairly unassuming, inoffensive man. "Perhaps you upset someone without realising it? I don't mean to suggest that you've actually done anything of an offensive nature, Mr Pouch, but people can be touchy about the smallest things."

"I don't think I've ever said or done anything that could possibly upset someone, or even mildly irritate them."

Churchill nodded. "Very well. We can only assume, then, that the assailant's anger was directed at the snowman. Was it a particularly good snowman?"

"Oh, yes. I always pride myself on building a good snowman. He stood about four feet tall, with coal for the eyes and a carrot for the nose, as you know. I spent quite a bit of time collecting tiny stones for his mouth to give him a nice, wide smile. Oh, and he had a lovely, colourful scarf, too. That appears to have disappeared. I can't see it anywhere."

"Perhaps the attacker took it," suggested Pemberley.

"A macabre trophy of some sort to remind himself of the terrible act he'd committed," added Churchill. "This could be someone with a twisted mind. The scarf will provide a useful piece of evidence, though, if we're able to find it in someone's possession. Can you please describe it for me, Mr Pouch?" She took her notebook from her handbag to note the description down.

"Brown, purple and green stripes. My three favourite colours."

"Very fine colours indeed."

"I think the culprit must have been walking down the lane there and spotted Mr Marzipan as he looked over the hedge," said Mr Pouch.

"Mr Marzipan?"

"That's what we called the snowman."

"I like marzipan." Churchill felt her mouth water at the very thought of it. There was some Christmas cake in a tin in her office and she couldn't wait to get back to it. She turned to Mr Pouch, eager to wrap things up. "You say someone could have spotted the snowman as they walked down the lane. Surely it would have been dark, would it not?"

"I think the offender must have walked past during the day and decided to come back after dark to beat Mr Marzipan to pieces."

"How terribly brutish," commented Churchill.

"I'm feeling quite upset about it," said Mr Pouch. "I know he was only a snowman, but…" His voice trailed off and he wiped his eyes with a gloved hand.

Churchill tightened her scarf and stamped her feet a little, trying to restore some warmth to her numb toes. "We have some clues," she said. "The culprit has left a lot of footprints."

"Which your dog is currently trampling all over," replied Mr Pouch.

"Call him over, Miss Pemberley," said Churchill. "He's ruining our evidence."

"Oswald!" Pemberley called out.

The scruffy little dog ignored her as he criss-crossed the garden, trying to catch snowflakes in his mouth.

"Oswald!" she called again.

"Never mind," said Churchill. "Let's get a good look at these footprints before the snow covers them again."

"It's quite creepy, isn't it?" commented Pemberley. "To think they're the footprints of someone who would willingly cause such destruction. Shall we measure them?"

"Good idea. Measuring tape at the ready, please."

"Measuring tape?"

"Don't you have a measuring tape in your handbag?"

"No, Mrs Churchill. Do you?"

"No, Miss Pemberley. I assumed you did."

"And I assumed you—"

"Yes, all right. I get the idea." Churchill opened her handbag and looked for something that would enable her to measure the footprint. "All I've got in here is a crochet needle. I suppose we could see how many crocheting needles the footprint is in width and length." She pulled it out of her bag, then bent down next to one of the snowy prints. "I would say that it's one-and-a-half crochet needles long and about half a crochet needle wide."

"The sole print looks interesting," said Pemberley. "It's ridged with horizontal stripes."

"So it is. Did you bring the camera with you?"

4

"No. Did you?"

"No, so we can't take a photograph of it, I'll make a quick sketch instead. This evidence won't be here for long. It'll be covered up by the new snowfall, then eventually melt." Churchill drew a rudimentary picture of the print, then watched Oswald flick snow over her boots as he dug excitedly in the snow. "At least someone's having fun this morning."

"He's full of beans because it's snowy and it's nearly Christmastime," said Pemberley.

"Yoo-hoo!" came a friendly call from the cottage door.

They turned to see a red-haired lady stepping out of the cottage in a thick overcoat and boots.

"Mrs *Thonnings*?" queried Churchill. "What on earth are you doing here?"

Mrs Thonnings and Mr Pouch exchanged a coy glance and Churchill immediately realised how foolish a question it had been. "Oh I see," she added. "The pair of you are... Yes, I see now." She made some arbitrary notes in her notebook. "Very good. Did you happen to see or hear anything out here last night, Mrs Thonnings?"

"I'm afraid not," she responded. "I slept like a log."

"All we've got to go on, then, is that this crime was committed between the hours of ten o'clock last night and sunrise this morning. What time was that?"

"Eight o'clock," said Pemberley.

Churchill wrote this down. "We have the scarf to look out for and we've measured the footprints." A thought occurred to her, and she turned back to the red-haired haberdasher. "Perhaps the assailant's ire was directed at you, Mrs Thonnings?"

"Me? No, that's impossible. Nobody knew I was here. Other than Mrs Higginbath, who's feeding my cat this morning."

"Can you think of anyone who may be upset about the... the *liaison* between the pair of you?"

"I suppose it could have been one of my jealous ex-lovers."

Churchill felt a little nauseous at the thought. "Anyone in particular?"

"Not really. They can all get a bit funny when you move on to someone new, can't they? That said, I don't think anyone knows that Bernard and I are an item yet."

"I see."

"Seeing as you're here, Mrs Churchill and Miss Pemberley, perhaps you'd like to come to my Christmas dinner party? I've got Mrs Dobinson coming in to do the cooking."

"That would be lovely, Mrs Thonnings. When is it?"

"This evening."

"This evening? It's something you've arranged at the last minute?"

"Oh, no. I began arranging it a long time ago. Back in October, in fact."

"Oh?"

"But there's space for two extras this evening."

"You haven't been able to fill all the spaces?"

"Yes, they were all filled in October, but Mrs Harris and Mrs Rumbold have dropped out."

"I see. So you didn't originally intend to invite us?"

"Well, I was going to, but then, you see, it was kind of a... a reciprocal invitation for people who have invited me to their Christmas dinners over the past few years." Mrs Thonnings gave an awkward grin.

Churchill felt herself bristling, then decided not to be offended, given that it was Christmastime and she was looking forward to some festive fun. "Thank you for your kind invitation, Mrs Thonnings. We'd be delighted to attend, wouldn't we, Miss Pemberley?"

"I think so."

"Oh, wonderful!" Mrs Thonnings clapped her hands together with glee. "I'll see you both at my house at six o'clock."

Chapter 2

CHURCHILL AND PEMBERLEY stopped off at the tea rooms to thaw out with hot tea and a plate of warm scones. Festive bunting hung from the ceiling and a Christmas tree sparkled next to the cake counter.

"I still shudder at the thought of what's been done to that snowman," said Churchill.

"Me too. I think it must have been one of Mrs Thonnings's ex-lovers."

"That's a strong possibility, but it doesn't account for the fact that Farmer Drumhead's snowman was brutally destroyed the night before. In that incident the snowman's flat cap was stolen from the scene. I think the two incidents must be linked."

"But who could be behind them?"

"That's for us to find out, isn't it, Pembers? Erm, what's Oswald eating? I thought he wasn't allowed titbits."

"He's not." Pemberley glanced down at him. "Where did you get that cake from, Oswald?"

"Oh, it was me," exclaimed a voice from behind them.

They turned to see a lady with a snub nose and a

freckled complexion buttoning up her blue coat. "I couldn't manage the rest of my coffee and walnut cake, and he was looking up at me with those big, adorable eyes. I couldn't resist it."

"He's not allowed cake!" snapped Pemberley.

"Is he not?" The lady's face fell. "I didn't realise that, sorry. It's just that I'm sure I've seen him in here before, and I've seen you," she nodded at Churchill, "slipping him small pieces of cake under the table. That's why I thought it would be all right."

Churchill felt Pemberley's sharp gaze turn on her. "Is that true, Mrs Churchill? Have you been feeding Oswald cake in here without me knowing?"

Churchill squirmed in her chair. "Very occasionally and always accidentally," she replied. "I find I can be a little careless sometimes when I've got a large slice of cake, and on very rare occasions a small piece may fall down onto the floor. Before I can retrieve it, he's snaffled it up. You know what Oswald's like; he has very quick reflexes. His little mouth gets there far quicker than my fingers ever could."

"It didn't look like that to me," said the lady. "In fact, it appeared quite deliberate on several occasions."

Churchill glared at the unknown woman, willing her to fall silent. "I don't believe we've met before," she said coldly.

"No, not properly, although I've seen you about. You're the detective ladies aren't you? Churchill and Pemberley."

"That's right." Churchill felt rather flattered that she had become so easily recognisable in the village. "And you are?"

"Mrs Marrowpip. I do like these tea rooms, don't you? In fact, I know you do because you're in here all the time."

"Not *all* the time," corrected Churchill. "We only pop

in when we need a little invigoration. We're extremely busy, aren't we, Miss Pemberley?"

"Sometimes."

"*Always.*" Churchill wasn't about to admit that the only case they were currently working on involved two vandalised snowmen.

"Well, you certainly eat a lot of cake," said Mrs Marrowpip. "I've noticed that."

"I do believe you were on your way out just now," said Churchill. "Don't let us hold you up, Mrs Marrowpip."

"Oh, you're not. I'm just—"

"Goodbye, then."

"Right. Yes. Goodbye."

Churchill spread the cream on her scone so firmly that it broke in half. "Darn it," she said, watching Mrs Marrowpip as she left the tea rooms. "What an annoying lady."

"You're only saying that because she said she'd seen you feeding cake to Oswald."

"That's not the case at all, Pembers! Anyone can see that she's an infuriating lady in general. There's no need for anyone to be that annoying. Anyway, we've a Christmas dinner to attend this evening. Are you looking forward to it?"

"Not especially."

"Why not?"

"I don't like last-minute invitations. I like to know about these things well in advance so I can prepare myself."

"I don't see what preparation could be required for a Christmas dinner with Mrs Thonnings. I'm looking forward to it. The Christmas dinner invitations have been rather thin on the ground this year."

"Have they?"

"Yes, haven't you found that?"

"No. There've been so many that I've had to turn some down."

"Which ones have you turned down?"

"Well, Mrs Higginbath's is one I shan't be attending this year."

"Oh, yes. I can't think of anything worse than having Christmas dinner with Mrs Higginbath. It would be funereal."

"And I can't make it to Inspector Mappin's Christmas dinner, either."

"Inspector Mappin? Why did *he* invite you to his Christmas dinner?"

"I don't know. I suppose we get on fairly well."

"Get on well? He's always accusing us of meddling!"

"He's always accusing *you* of meddling, Mrs Churchill. I think he knows I'm just an innocent bystander most of the time."

"What nonsense. You make it sound as though I'm troublesome, Pembers. I'm not troublesome at all. Just think of all the cases we've solved in the past year or two. And how many has he solved? None!"

Churchill bit into her scone and concentrated on enjoying the perfect combination of jam and cream while trying not to dwell on the fact she hadn't been invited to as many Christmas dinners as her trusty assistant. The invitation to Mrs Thonnings's Christmas dinner party had only been made because two other guests had dropped out.

Night had fallen by the time Churchill, Pemberley and Oswald wended their way through the snow to Mrs Thonnings's cottage. It was tucked away in a pretty lane just off the high street. Lights on Christmas trees twinkled in the windows and colourful Christmas wreaths hung on every door.

"Isn't Christmastime lovely, Pembers? Are those carol singers I hear?"

The two ladies paused as the strain of 'Deck the Halls' grew louder. From around the corner came the village choir, all carrying lanterns and wearing hats, gloves and coats over their robes.

People stepped out of their doors to listen, while Oswald ran around, exuberantly sniffing at boots and receiving many pats on the head.

"Look at that, Pembers. What a lovely Christmas scene. Couldn't you just paint it?"

"I'm no good at painting."

"Me neither. I could write a poem about it, though. I can feel one coming on, in fact. I shall have to put pen to paper when I get home this evening."

Mrs Thonnings flung open her cottage door in response to their knock and greeted them with a wide smile. She wore a festive, scarlet and green patterned blouse, and her cheeks were almost as red as her hair.

"Come in, ladies! Come in, come in. Mrs Churchill and Miss Pemberley – my two favouritist lady detectives!"

"Do you think she's already been at the Christmas sherry, Pembers?" whispered Churchill as they followed her inside the warm cottage.

A twinkling Christmas tree stood by the window in the front room, and Mr Pouch warmed himself in front of the fire. He wore a cosy, cable-knit cardigan and held a glass of whisky in his hand. "Good evening, ladies. Have you found out who destroyed my snowman yet?"

"Not yet, Mr Pouch. We were only called out to assist you this morning."

"Was it really only this morning? An awful lot of time seems to pass when something so terrible happens, doesn't it?"

"It does indeed."

"This is Miss Broadspoon," said Mrs Thonnings, gesturing to a small lady who slumped on the sofa.

"How nice to meet, you, Miss Broadspoon," said Churchill.

"Likewise," she replied. Her thick-lensed spectacles gave her a myopic appearance, and she had a large nose and grey, wavy hair. "I would get up, but I can't very easily because of my hip."

"Stay right where you are, Miss Broadspoon. No need to get up on our account."

"I think a bit of cold must have got into it."

"Into your hip?"

"Yes. Happens this time every year. It often completely ruins my Christmas."

"I'm sorry to hear it."

"I'll survive. The sherry's helping."

"That reminds me," said Mrs Thonnings, turning to Churchill and Pemberley. "Would you like a sherry?"

"We'd love one. Thank you, Mrs Thonnings."

Their hostess went off to fetch the drinks while the two detectives made themselves comfortable next to Miss Broadspoon. Oswald lay down in front of the fire, next to Mr Pouch.

"So is this all of us, then?" queried Churchill. "Five?"

"Oh, no. Gladys has invited a few more," replied Mr Pouch. "Mrs Higginbath is among them, I believe."

Churchill gave a small cough in place of the groan she wanted to emit. "Who else?" she asked. "I hope you're

13

about to mention someone who's the life and soul of the party."

"Well, if you want someone who's the life and soul of the party, I suppose I'm a good contender," he replied.

Churchill coughed again. "Are you really?"

"Oh, yes. I've a few funny tales I can regale you with over dinner."

"I'm looking forward to it."

The doorbell rang.

"Here's Mrs Higginbath!" exclaimed Mrs Thonnings, leading the tall, broad-framed librarian into the front room. Her long grey hair hung down either side of her scowling face like a pair of curtains. "My most favouritist librarian in the whole of Dorset!" added Mrs Thonnings.

"Merry Christmas, Mrs Higginbath!" said Churchill, forcing a smile onto her face.

"And you, too, Mrs Churchill," replied the stern librarian. "I wasn't made aware that you were coming this evening."

"Oh, that's because Mrs Harris and Mrs Rumbold dropped out," said Mrs Thonnings.

"That's a shame. I was looking forward to seeing them both."

Churchill felt a distinct urge for sherry. She hoped beyond hope it would arrive soon.

The doorbell rang again.

"Oh!" exclaimed Mrs Thonnings, as if surprised that someone else should be calling at her door. "I wonder who that is?"

"I hope it's someone nice," muttered Pemberley.

Mrs Thonnings returned to the room accompanied by a bald-headed man with dark eyes and a neat, grey moustache. He wore a smart, dark suit with a bow tie and held a bottle of expensive-looking brandy.

"Merry Christmas!" he exclaimed. "How lovely to see you all here."

His voice was deep and mellifluous and made Churchill think of chocolate melting into a mug of warm milk.

"Merry Christmas to you, too," she said with a smile.

"This is Dr Jonathan Sillifant," said Mrs Thonnings. "He's been a doctor in Compton Poppleford for almost fifty years and knows the full medical details of just about everybody in the village. Wouldn't you say so, Doctor?"

"Yes, that's right. Pretty much every single medical condition is inscribed upon my mind. However, my professional obligation means I couldn't possibly share them with anybody."

"No, of course not," said Mrs Thonnings. "But perhaps a little later, after dinner, you might let a few things slip?" She gave a wink.

"I never let anything slip, Mrs Thonnings."

"Just occasionally, you do."

"I shan't comment any further." He turned to Miss Broadspoon. "It's wonderful to see one of my favourite patients here this evening. How's the complaint, Miss Broadspoon?"

"Oh, it's much better, thank you, Doctor. It's my hip that's bothering me now."

"I'm very sorry to hear it. Perhaps we can consult a little later this evening?"

"Thank you, Doctor."

"Now, that's enough," said Mr Thonnings. "You're not at work now, Doctor. You're here to enjoy yourself."

"I can't help but notice that the delightful Mrs Churchill and Miss Pemberley are without a drink," he remarked. "How about a bit of my brandy?" He handed Mrs Thonnings the bottle.

"They're having sherry."

"Oh, I see."

"I've changed my mind," said Churchill. "I shall have some brandy."

"I still want sherry," said Pemberley.

The doorbell rang again.

"That'll be my final guest!" Mrs Thonnings skipped off to answer the door.

Doctor Sillifant hitched his trousers above the knee and seated himself in an armchair. Moments later, a lady with a snub nose and a freckled complexion appeared with the host. "Here's Mrs Marrowpip!" announced Mrs Thonnings. "Now, let the festivities begin!"

Chapter 3

"Now that everybody is here, we can play our first parlour game," said Mrs Thonnings once she had handed out the drinks.

"First parlour game?" queried Mrs Higginbath. "There's going to be more than one?"

"Absolutely! Now, seeing as I'm a happy little haberdasher, our first game will be Hunt the Thimble."

"How do you play that?" asked Miss Broadspoon.

"You all go out of the room, and I hide my thimble somewhere." Mrs Thonnings held up the shiny silver thimble to show them what it looked like. "Then you all come back in and look for it."

"Where were you going to hide it?" asked Mrs Marrowpip.

Dr Sillifant laughed. "Don't think you're going to get away with that sort of trick question! Come on, everybody. Let's leave the room while Mrs Thonnings hides her thimble."

Churchill and Pemberley rose to their feet and followed

the others out into the hallway. Mrs Thonnings shut the door on them.

"I do love a good game of Hunt the Thimble," said Mr Pouch. "Sometimes Gladys and I like to play it with just the two of us. She's extremely good at hiding things, you know. She knows all the best places."

"What sort of places?" asked Mrs Marrowpip.

"I don't want to be giving you any hints."

"I think you've got a distinct advantage over the rest of us, Pouch," said Dr Sillifant. "If you and Mrs Thonnings regularly play Hunt the Thimble, you must already know all the best hiding places."

"Oh, I wouldn't know about that. Gladys has the uncanny ability to find new hiding places every time. I don't believe she's ever used the same hiding place more than once."

"That sounds very impressive indeed," said the doctor.

"How long does it take to hide a thimble?" moaned Mrs Higginbath.

"Perhaps she's hiding it under the floorboards?" said Miss Broadspoon.

"Oh, hello! And who does this little fellow belong to?" asked Dr Sillifant, bending down to pat Oswald's head. "What a lovely chap."

"He's mine," said Churchill, batting her eyelashes.

"Actually, he's mine," said Pemberley.

"Both of ours. We both look after him."

"But he belongs to *me*," said Pemberley.

"Well, he's quite delightful," said the doctor. "If you're not careful, ladies, I shall tuck him inside my jacket and take him home with me."

"That would be extremely naughty of you, Doctor," said Churchill with what she hoped was a winning smile.

He chuckled.

The door to the front room opened. "Come in, come in!" said Mrs Thonnings, grinning from ear to ear. "You'll never find it!"

"Then what's the point in playing?" asked Mrs Higginbath.

"Oh, don't be so miserable, Mrs Higginbath. It's Christmas! Now then, everybody. Hunt high and low!"

Churchill peeked behind the figurines on the mantelpiece and felt disappointed by the absence of the thimble. She saw Pemberley pulling books out of a small bookcase and Dr Sillifant lifting the cushions on the sofa. Mrs Higginbath peered under the rug and Miss Broadspoon had pulled out a drawer from the writing table. Mrs Marrowpip shook the curtains. "Is it balanced on the curtain rail?" she asked.

"I don't think so," said Mr Pouch, looking behind a picture. "She's already used that hiding place."

After a while, everybody swapped positions and searched areas that had already been checked.

Growing increasingly bored, Churchill hankered after another brandy.

"Where is it?" said Mrs Higginbath. "I give up."

"The others haven't given up," said Mrs Thonnings.

"I'm giving up," said Miss Broadspoon, slumping onto the sofa.

"And me," said Mr Pouch, sitting next to her.

"But you've hardly begun looking yet!" said Dr Sillifant.

"Perhaps you could give us a clue?" said Churchill.

"I don't give clues," replied Mrs Thonnings.

Now three guests had given up, Churchill felt more determined to find the thimble herself.

Mrs Marrowpip was keener still. "Get up off the sofa,"

she commanded the guests sitting there. "I want to have a proper look."

"I've already checked it," said Mrs Higginbath.

"But I want to check it myself."

The three guests reluctantly got up and Mrs Marrowpip began pulling the cushions aside.

"Careful, Enid!" exclaimed Mrs Thonnings, as a sofa cushion narrowly missed the lamp on the side table. "There's no need to go ransacking the place."

"I want to be the first to find the thimble!"

Becoming even more determined, Churchill began taking the back off the carriage clock.

"Where *is* the darned thing?" said Dr Sillifant, unbuttoning a cushion cover.

Oswald barked and scampered happily around the room.

Churchill examined every ornament on the Christmas tree, searching among the shiny glass baubles, striped sticks of candy and tinkling gold bells for the elusive thimble.

"Peekaboo," said a rich-toned voice. Dr Sillifant's face loomed into view through the branches.

"Oh, Doctor!" giggled Churchill. "You startled me!"

"Looks like we had the same idea," he said. "You'd better not find it before I do."

"We'll see about that!"

The search continued until Churchill's back ached from stooping over. She felt a strain in her eyes from peering into things. She wanted to give up and sit down with a drink, but she didn't want anyone else to find the thimble. She peeped into the lamp and dazzled herself with the bulb. "You're very good at hiding things, Mrs Thonnings."

"I know. Fun, isn't it?"

"You could call it that, I suppose."

"Please stop pulling up the carpet, Enid," pleaded Mrs Thonnings. "It'll get all crumpled."

"I need to look under the floorboards."

"No, you don't. I haven't hidden the thimble under the floorboards."

Mrs Marrowpip replaced the corner of the carpet and stamped it down with her foot. Then she marched over to the bookcase and began hauling the books off in armfuls.

Dr Sillifant laughed. "What's so funny?" asked Mrs Higginbath.

"I can see it," he said.

"See it? How can you possibly see it? We've searched the entire room!"

Dr Sillifant laughed again and pointed at Oswald, who sat on the hearth rug. "He's got it between his teeth."

"Oh, well done, Oswald!" exclaimed Pemberley. "You found the thimble!"

Mrs Thonnings frowned. "It wasn't supposed to be found by the dog," she grumbled.

"Why not?" queried Pemberley.

"Because he's not one of my guests."

"Of course he's one of your guests! He's a dog guest. And he waited very patiently with the rest of us in the hallway while you were hiding it."

"Where was it before he found it?" asked Mrs Higginbath.

"I'm not prepared to say," replied Mrs Thonnings. "I shall have to hide it again now. And the dog isn't playing this time!"

The second game of Hunt the Thimble came to an end after Miss Broadspoon complained she was sitting on something uncomfortable and retrieved it from beneath a sofa cushion.

"Just like the princess and the pea," chuckled Dr Sillifant. "Now we know you're a true princess, Miss Broadspoon."

She turned bashful and Churchill felt a twinge of envy. It was accompanied by a twinge of hunger.

"We don't have time for any more parlour games," said Mrs Thonnings. "But we can play some more after dinner if you like?"

"Let's decide after we've eaten," said the doctor.

"Oh all right then. In that case, it's dinner time!" announced the host.

Churchill was first to the table.

Once everyone was seated, pear-shaped Mrs Dobinson brought in the first course. Churchill was disappointed to discover two slices of melon on her plate rather than something a little more filling.

"We must pull our Christmas crackers first," said Mrs Thonnings, handing them out. Churchill pulled hers with Dr Sillifant and managed to win the paper hat, riddle and bejewelled plastic ring.

"I've got a comb," said Mrs Thonnings.

"Rather more useful than mine," said Mr Pouch. "A stick of chalk. I could give it to my sister, I suppose." Churchill wondered what Mr Pouch's sister would want with a piece of chalk.

"How's business, Bernard?" the doctor asked, as everyone tucked into the melon course.

The corners of Mr Pouch's mouth turned downwards. "Not very well at all. I'm shutting up shop."

"Oh dear. Why's that?"

"Not enough customers."

"What is your business?" asked Churchill.

"I run a hardware shop."

"The one on the high street?"

"No, that one's mine," said Mrs Marrowpip.

"You own the hardware store on the high street, Mrs Marrowpip?" asked Churchill.

"That's right. I have done for years. It began with my husband and I, and then he… Well, it's just me now."

"I'm sorry to hear that."

"I'm better off without him actually."

"I see."

"My shop's on Dogwood Street," said Mr Pouch.

"Where's that?" asked Churchill, realising how much local knowledge she still had to acquire.

"A little alleyway near the railway station."

"I've never heard of it."

"That's part of the problem," said Mrs Thonnings. "Nobody knows it's there. He has hardly any customers."

"I've been advertising in the *Compton Poppleford Gazette*," said Mr Pouch. "But it's not enough."

"No, it wouldn't be," said Dr Sillifant. "You need people passing by your front door, I'm afraid. That's the advantage Mrs Marrowpip has. People are passing her shop all the time. That's how she gets her business."

"Thank you for pointing that out, Doctor," replied Mr Pouch sadly.

"You opened your shop in the wrong place," Mrs Marrowpip added. "It's obvious that you shouldn't open a shop on a little street nobody ever walks down. I've only ever walked down Dogwood Street once, and that was by mistake. As soon as I realised it, I turned back, so I didn't even get as far as your shop. You've only got yourself to blame, Mr Pouch. Why on earth did you think anybody would go out of their way to visit your shop when there's a perfectly good one on the high street?"

"Steady on, Mrs Marrowpip," said Dr Sillifant. "I'm quite sure the good chap's realised his mistake by now. There's no need for you to go putting the boot in."

Mr Pouch pushed a piece of melon into his mouth and said nothing.

"Poor Bernard's going to have to sack his staff tomorrow," said Mrs Thonnings. "They're all going to lose their jobs – and just before Christmas, as well."

Everybody stared at Mr Pouch, as if reprimanding him for his poor judgement.

Churchill felt a little bit sorry for him. "Never mind," she said. "I think it's most commendable of you to run your own business, Mr Pouch. I'm sure another opportunity will arise for you soon."

"Thank you, Mrs Churchill."

Bowls of hot onion soup were brought in with chunks of warm, crusty bread. Roasted goose with a range of vegetables, side dishes, gravy and sauces soon followed. The wine flowed.

Churchill felt pleasantly warm and relaxed. She sat back in her chair, adjusted her paper hat, and decided she could listen to Dr Sillifant's soothing voice all night. She felt so relaxed that she even managed to laugh at one of Mrs Higginbath's library jokes.

"Mrs Dobinson has put together a delightful cheeseboard," said Mrs Thonnings. "But before that, it's time for my famous plum pudding!"

Everybody clapped excitedly.

"Yummy!" said Dr Sillifant.

"Why is it famous?" asked Mrs Marrowpip.

"It just is," responded Mrs Higginbath.

Mrs Thonnings went into the kitchen and returned with the plum pudding proudly presented on a silver serving platter. A sprig of holly garnished the top, and a delicious waft of brandy and spiced fruits made Churchill's mouth water. Mrs Thonnings picked up a silver serving spoon and set to work dishing out the pudding.

"That serving's too large for me," grumbled Miss Broadspoon.

"Very well," said Mrs Thonnings. "I'll give it to Bernard."

"Too small for me," said Mr Pouch.

"I'll have it," said Mrs Marrowpip. "Actually, no I won't. I'll have that other one you've just done."

"That's mine," said Mr Pouch.

"It was supposed to be Mrs Churchill's," said Mrs Thonnings, growing flustered.

"Whose is this that I've got?" asked Dr Sillifant.

"Miss Broadspoon's," said Mr Pouch.

"It's no smaller than the last one," she moaned as it was passed to her.

"I do enjoy a good game of Pass the Pudding," said Dr Sillifant with a chuckle.

Eventually, everyone had a serving they seemed pleased with.

"This is an absolute delight," commented Mr Pouch.

"Simply wonderful," added Mrs Higginbath.

"Exquisite," said Dr Sillifant.

Churchill felt she should chip in. "Marvellously delicious."

"Are you alright, Enid?" asked Mrs Thonnings.

"Not really," she replied. "I think I need a little air. Do please excuse me." Mrs Marrowpip got up from the table and left the room.

"Biliousness," commented Dr Sillifant. "It can be a terrible problem at this time of year when we're all indulging in a little feasting."

"You're so knowledgeable, Doctor," said Churchill.

"About biliousness?" queried Pemberley.

"About everything to do with doctoring and medical things," she replied. "How do you keep it all in your head, Doctor?"

He chuckled and adjusted his bow tie. "Many years of training and practising, Mrs Churchill. It's that simple."

"Ah, but it's not simple, is it? It's absolutely, wonderfully and completely clever."

Mrs Dobinson came into the room and whispered in Mrs Thonnings's ear.

"Oh, goodness!" Mrs Thonnings leapt to her feet.

"What is it, Gladys?" asked Mr Pouch.

"Poor Enid has been taken unwell. I must go to her."

"I shall come, too," said the doctor, standing abruptly.

The pair dashed out of the room.

"Oh dear," said Mrs Higginbath. "Perhaps it's a little more than a hint of biliousness."

"I hope she's all right," said Miss Broadspoon. "It's no fun being ill at Christmastime. I should know."

"At least she has Dr Sillifant to tend to her," said Churchill. "She's in good hands."

Moments later, Mrs Thonnings returned, her face pale.

"Gladys?" ventured Mr Pouch.

"Oh, goodness… Oh, deary me…" She stumbled as she tried to get to her chair.

"What is it, Mrs Thonnings?" asked Churchill, helping her into her seat. "How's Mrs Marrowpip?"

"It's terrible news!" she wailed. "She's dead!"

Chapter 4

TWENTY MINUTES LATER, brown-whiskered Inspector Mappin sat at Mrs Thonnings's dining table. The plates and dishes had been cleared away, and everyone had removed their paper party hats.

"It's always a shame when a Christmas party ends in tragedy," he said. "Especially as I'll need to question you all in great detail now. You'll have to forget about all the fun you were having."

"What a terrible end to a delightful party," commented Miss Broadspoon.

"I'd have described it as a *tolerable* party," said Mrs Higginbath, "but I never imagined it would sink to such depths."

Mrs Thonnings sobbed into a handkerchief. Mr Pouch sat next to her, his arm across her shoulders.

"I was quite enjoying it," said Pemberley.

"Me too," added Churchill.

"Dr Sillifant is still speaking to the police doctor, but I think the two are already in agreement that Mrs Marrowpip was poisoned," said Inspector Mappin.

"Poisoned? What by?" asked Miss Broadspoon.

"Poison," replied Mrs Higginbath.

"But where was it? In the food?"

"It must have been in the pudding," said Churchill. "Mrs Marrowpip went swiftly downhill after a mere mouthful."

"It wouldn't do to speculate at the current time," said the inspector, turning to a fresh page in his notebook. "It's important that we gather all the facts and evidence first."

"This is all my fault!" wailed Mrs Thonnings.

"It's only your fault if you put the poison in Mrs Marrowpip's pudding," said Mr Pouch. "And I'm quite sure that you didn't."

"Then the obvious question is, who did?" asked Inspector Mappin. He peered closely at each of them, as if scrutinising their faces for signs of guilt.

"Have you spoken to the lady who cooked the food, Inspector?" asked Churchill.

"No. I assumed it was Mrs Thonnings who'd cooked the food. Who's the lady?"

"Mrs Dobinson," said Mrs Thonnings. "But she wouldn't have put poison in the pudding, I was the one who cooked the pudding!"

"I'll speak to Mrs Dobinson first," said the inspector. "The rest of you can wait here while I go to the kitchen." He left the room.

"Are we expected to just sit here until he's finished?" queried Mrs Higginbath.

"Of course," replied Mr Pouch. "That poor lady has just been poisoned. Nobody should be allowed to go anywhere until the inspector has a good grasp of the situation."

"Which could take a while," said Churchill. "I don't

think he's ever grasped anything in the time I've known him."

"That's a little unfair, Mrs Churchill," said the stern-faced librarian. "Inspector Mappin is an extremely able and conscientious police officer."

"Good. Then hopefully this case will be solved within a matter of hours."

"I'm going to be the one everybody points the finger at," said Mrs Thonnings. "I just know it!"

"Not at all, Gladys," said Mr Pouch. "All of us were in the room when it happened. Any one of us could have put the poison into Mrs Marrowpip's plum pudding."

Dr Sillifant walked back into the room, sat down and sombrely wiped his brow.

"If the poisoning happened in this very room, why didn't anyone see anything?" asked Mrs Thonnings. "I just know that I'm going to be blamed because I was the one who cooked the pudding."

"Maybe the poison was in something else?" suggested Miss Broadspoon.

"But it can't have been, it was the pudding she took ill from, I'm sure of it." Mrs Thonnings burst into another round of sobs.

"There, there," said Mr Pouch, patting her on the back. "Even if you do become the main suspect, don't forget who my brother is. The honourable Joseph Pouch KC will soon have something to say about it. I'll make sure of that."

"Your brother is a judge?" asked Churchill.

"Oh, yes," replied Mr Pouch. "One of the most accomplished judges in the land. He's sent twelve men to the gallows in the past year alone."

"Ugh," said Pemberley.

"I don't know what you're protesting about," said Mr

Pouch. "Every one of those men was a criminal, and my brother dealt with them all fairly and justly."

Mrs Thonnings gave out another wail. "That's what's going to happen to me! I'll be sent to the gallows!"

"No you won't, Gladys. Joseph will help you."

"Surely it's the jury that decides whether somebody's guilty of murder or not?" said Dr Sillifant.

"Ah, but the judge has the final word," said Mr Pouch. "Especially when it comes to the gallows." He turned back to Mrs Thonnings. "Even if the jury did find you guilty, I would ensure that Joseph had you excused from the gallows. It would just be a long time in prison instead."

"But I haven't done anything!" wailed Mrs Thonnings.

"No, of course you haven't. I was speaking hypo-thetically."

"This is all too upsetting," said Miss Broadspoon. "I'm getting one of my heads."

"One of your heads?" queried Churchill.

"Yes. I always get them when things like this happen."

"You've got more than one head?" asked Pemberley.

"Of course not, Miss Pemberley," Churchill responded. "I believe she's describing a headache."

"It's more than a headache," said Miss Broadspoon. "It feels as if my brain has been spliced in two by an axe."

"Oh, yuck!" exclaimed Pemberley. She picked up Oswald and cuddled him for comfort.

"Would you like to have a lie down, Miss Broad-spoon?" asked Dr Sillifant. "I understand this must be a very upsetting time for you. Perhaps you could have a little rest on the sofa in the front room. Would that be all right, Mrs Thonnings?"

The haberdasher nodded and gave another loud sob.

As Dr Sillifant escorted Miss Broadspoon out of the

room, Churchill wondered what she could do to earn herself a little medical attention.

Everyone sat in silence for a while, then Churchill felt the need to make conversation. "How's the library, Mrs Higginbath?"

"Still standing, the last time I saw it."

"Good. Well, that's something, I suppose."

Inspector Mappin returned to the room. "I've had a word with Mrs Dobinson, and I will now speak to each of you in turn."

"When can we go home?" asked Mrs Higginbath.

"After I've spoken to you all." He turned to Mrs Thonnings. "Do you keep any poison in the house?"

"Poison? No!"

"Not even rat poison?"

"Oh, yes. I have some rat poison."

"And where's that normally kept?"

"In the cupboard under the stairs, Inspector. Oh, no! Now you're going to suspect me even more, aren't you?"

"At the present time, Mrs Thonnings, I'm forced to suspect everybody who was present at this party."

"Even us, Inspector?" queried Churchill.

"Absolutely, Mrs Churchill. Just because you claim to be detectives yourselves, it doesn't mean that you're incapable of committing a crime. Everybody will be treated as a suspect until I have firm evidence that points directly to one or more individuals."

"Oh, goodness," said Churchill. "How very strict, Inspector."

"It's a very serious matter, Mrs Churchill. Now then," he turned to Mrs Thonnings, "perhaps you can show me where you keep that poison?"

Chapter 5

"GOOD GRIEF, PEMBERS," said Churchill as the pair sat in their office the following morning. "What an awful evening. I'm never spending Christmas with Mrs Thonnings again."

"Her Christmas dinners are quite often eventful, but that's the first time anyone has been murdered at one of them."

"Which of the guests did it, do you think?"

Pemberley shook her head. "It's impossible to believe that any of them did it."

"What about Mrs Higginbath? There was a murderous expression on her face at several points during the evening."

"Mrs Higginbath's bark is much worse than her bite. You must know that by now, Mrs Churchill. She's as gentle as a puppy once you get to know her."

Churchill snorted and picked up a mince pie from the plate in front of her. "If Mrs Higginbath were provoked, I think she could easily poison someone."

"I've known her a long time. For... no, I won't say how many years. Let's just say that I was at school with her.

Anyway, I really don't think she would sink so low as to poison someone."

"Fair enough. So, who do you think did it?"

"Well, I'm not too sure about that doctor. You know what they say about doctors."

"What do they say about doctors?"

"They say that when it comes to poisoning, doctors are the likeliest suspects because they can get hold of poison very easily."

"While I can see the logic behind that theory, Pembers, it certainly couldn't be the case where Dr Sillifant is concerned."

"Why not?"

"It just couldn't. Dr Sillifant isn't the type."

"You've got a soft spot for him, Mrs Churchill. I can tell."

"Nonsense!" Churchill felt her face heat up. "I have no spot whatsoever, soft or otherwise. Let's set up our incident board once I've finished this mince pie."

The two ladies spent a good hour pinning up notes and pictures, attaching them together with pieces of string.

Eventually, Churchill stepped back to admire their work. "I'm always amazed by your ability to find pictures of people, Pembers."

"I like cutting their pictures out from the newspaper and various bulletins. Then I file them away. You never know when they'll come in handy."

"Mrs Higginbath looks very youthful on our board."

"Yes, that picture was taken when she was appointed to her first position at the library."

"A good number of years ago now, I suspect. She had quite pleasant facial features back then, didn't she? I wonder what happened in the intervening years for her to have ended up with the scowling visage we're so accustomed to." She examined the incident board again. "Interesting to see Dr Sillifant with some hair in that picture. Where did you find it?"

"A leaflet he put through everyone's doors when he set up his own practice. He looks quite handsome, wouldn't you say, Mrs Churchill?"

"I really couldn't say ..." Churchill felt her face grow hot again. "Why are you asking me that, Pembers?"

"It would have been easy for Dr Sillifant to walk into a pharmacy and obtain the poison," Pemberley commented, ignoring Churchill's question. "But what we need to understand is his motive."

"Oh, there couldn't possibly be one, I feel sure of it. Now, Miss Broadspoon. She's a dark horse, isn't she? What do we know about her?"

"She used to be good friends with Mrs Marrowpip and Mrs Higginbath, but there was some sort of falling out."

"What about?"

"I don't know. It was probably complicated; it usually is. You know the old saying, 'Two's company, three's a crowd.' It was inevitable that one of them would be pushed out for some reason or another."

"You think Mrs Marrowpip and Mrs Higginbath bore Miss Broadspoon a grudge?"

"Yes, I think so. Or the other way round, maybe. Or both ways."

"Goodness. Not a very sensible combination of guests for a Christmas dinner, then."

"Mrs Thonnings often invites the wrong people. One year she invited Farmer Firegrind and Mr Beaufort-Wallis. Those two in the same room as each other! Can you imagine?"

"No I can't, Pembers, because I've no idea who either might be. Anyway, it suffices to say that she doesn't choose her guests particularly well, and someone's been murdered as a result."

"There's always the possibility that Mrs Thonnings is the poisoner, Mrs Churchill."

"Golly, Pembers! What a thought!"

"I don't think she would've done it, though."

"How do you know that? She certainly had the means, because she was the one who made the plum pudding. It would have been very easy to put poison in that, I should imagine."

"But if she'd put the poison into the entire pudding we'd all have been poisoned, wouldn't we?"

"That's a good point. If she was targeting someone in particular, she wouldn't have put the poison into the whole plum pudding. What you mean, Pembers, is that someone poisoned only Mrs Marrowpip's portion of plum pudding."

"That's exactly what I mean."

"But how on earth could someone have done that? It could only have happened once Mrs Thonnings had served the plum pudding up and given everyone their bowls."

"Maybe Mrs Thonnings put the poison into one of the bowls and then ensured it was the bowl that Mrs Marrowpip received."

"Excellent! That's exactly what must have happened. But why would she do that?"

"I don't believe she would do that. Neither do I think she had any reason to do that. Besides, don't you remember how all the plum pudding portions got mixed up?"

"Yes, I remember now! Miss Broadspoon moaned hers was too large, which meant that someone else had it, and so on. Can you recall the exact chain of events, Pembers?"

"Unfortunately, I can't."

"Me neither." Churchill screwed her eyes shut and tried to picture the scene again. "It's no use," she said, opening them again. "We can only assume that, amid the plum pudding confusion, someone dropped the poison into Mrs Marrowpip's portion."

"I don't think Mrs Thonnings did it," said Pemberley. "I can't imagine her poisoning someone at her own Christmas dinner. If she'd wanted to murder Mrs Marrowpip, I think she would have done it at another time and in another place. Not in her own home."

"Good point. And why would she want to murder Mrs Marrowpip, anyway?"

"I've no idea."

"Me neither. Let's move on to her man friend, Mr Pouch. What's he got against Mrs Marrowpip?"

"She was rude to him about his shop."

"That's right, she was. Maybe he was envious of her because she has a large, successful hardware shop on the high street and he has a small, rubbish one on a street no one ever goes down. Then, to rub salt into the wounds, she mocked him for it."

"I could understand why he'd want to poison her."

"Ah, but the poisoning would have required premeditation, wouldn't it? One doesn't simply carry a dose of deadly poison in one's pocket just in case one becomes offended by an obnoxious dinner party guest."

"Some people might."

"I suppose we can't rule it out." Churchill sighed. "All this thinking is making me hungry and thirsty. Shall we have a break for tea and mince pies?"

· · ·

Oswald tidied up the crumbs beneath Churchill's desk as she sipped her tea and leafed through the *Compton Poppleford Gazette*. "Mrs Marrowpip's death has received a lot of coverage," she commented. "And as usual, half of it's wrong. How do these newspaper reporters and editors get away with it? They've put here that Mrs Thonnings is forty-two. I think they probably need to double that and take away ten."

"She can't be that old."

"She's certainly not forty-two. I think she's been telling that disreputable news reporter, Smithy Miggins, a few porkies." An advert caught Churchill's eye. "This looks like a bit of fun, Pembers. The Compton Poppleford Christmas Snowman Competition. 'All entries must be constructed by Christmas Eve. Judging will be carried out by the Mayor of Compton Poppleford and Inspector Mappin.' Inspector Mappin?! What does *he* know about snowmen?"

"As much as the next person, I suppose. The snow in this country never hangs around long enough for anyone to become an expert."

"I suppose if we can forget about who's judging it, it could be a bit of fun. The prize is ten pounds. Golly, that's a fair amount. Do you think you'll enter it, Pembers?"

They both started as the telephone on Pemberley's desk rang. Churchill listened intently as Pemberley spoke to the person at the other end.

"Yes... right... Thank you for letting us know, Mrs Craythorne. We'll be on our way soon." Pemberley replaced the receiver.

"Who was that?" asked Churchill.

"Doreen Craythorne, and she's terribly upset. Her snowman's been attacked. Primrose Lane yesterday evening. He was toppled and crushed, and his five brass buttons were stolen."

"Oh dear. We'd better pay her a visit. The trouble is, we have a proper case to work on now, so we don't really have time to find the person who's smashing up snowmen."

"But we've started the case, Mrs Churchill. We must do our best to finish it."

Chapter 6

CHURCHILL AND PEMBERLEY joined Mrs Craythorne in the garden of her terraced house near the church. Sunshine glistened on the snow and the sky was a bright blue. An otherwise pretty scene if it hadn't been for the crumpled remains of the snowman.

"I only made him yesterday," said Mrs Craythorne with a sniff. She wore a thick fur coat and a large fur hat. "And by the evening he'd been destroyed."

"What time in the evening?" asked Churchill.

"I got a knock on the door just after nine."

"The assailant knocked on the door?"

"Yes and I couldn't tell you who it was because they ran away again before I got there."

"Why did they knock?"

"They left an old ash bucket on the doorstep. It's one I'd finished with and left in the garden."

"And it was on your doorstep?"

"That's right. I thought it was a practical joke of some sort, so I fetched my torch, put my boots on, picked up the bucket and took it back round to the garden. It was then that I spotted these footprints."

Churchill surveyed them. "Ah, yes. These look familiar. Take some photographs please, Miss Pemberley."

"Certainly. I remembered to bring the camera this time."

"Good."

"The footprints look familiar?" Mrs Craythorne queried.

"Yes. We saw the same prints in Mr Pouch's garden."

"Was an ash bucket left on his doorstep?"

"No. That seems to be a new tactic."

"You'll need to come and take a look at it." She led the two old ladies over to a rusty bucket standing by the rear doorstep of her house. "I peered inside and got the shock of my life. Go on, lift the lid."

"Really?" Churchill hesitated, unsure what to expect.

"Just look inside, Mrs Churchill. You won't believe it!"

"Won't I?"

Churchill cautiously bent down and reached a gloved hand towards the wooden handle of the ash bucket lid. She raised it slowly.

As soon as she saw what was inside, she shrieked and recoiled. Staring back up at her, with its dark coal eyes, was the disembodied head of a snowman.

Churchill dropped the lid into the snow. "Oh goodness! Oh my days! I wasn't expecting that. What sort of a brute would do such a thing?"

"I didn't sleep a wink last night," said Mrs Craythorne.

"I'm not surprised! Miss Pemberley, please take a photograph of this barbarism."

"Oh, I couldn't possibly." She stood ten feet away.

"We need a visual record for our case notes! He'll start melting as soon as the thaw comes." Churchill cautiously peered into the bucket again. "In fact, his forehead's already looking a bit watery in this morning's sunshine. Come along, Miss Pemberley. Then we can be on our way."

"I can't and I won't."

"All right then. Hand me the camera and I'll do it." Churchill turned to Mrs Craythorne. "You must excuse us, we're still a little shaken up after an unfortunate incident at a friend's Christmas dinner last night."

"I heard all about that. Mrs Marrowpip was poisoned with a piece of plum pudding, wasn't she? Awful. The attack on my snowman is nothing compared to that."

"Did you know Mrs Marrowpip at all?"

"Reasonably well. She ran the hardware shop, didn't she? I wonder what's going to happen with the shop now. She was a nice lady, but she was never the same after her husband left."

"Her husband left? How very sad. Was it a recent event?"

"About five years ago," said Mrs Craythorne. "He ran off with another woman."

"Gosh! Poor Mrs Marrowpip must have been dreadfully upset."

"She was. She was fixated on exacting her revenge for a good while."

"Was she indeed? What sort of revenge?"

"She chopped up a pair of his trousers and set fire to his shed."

"Cripes."

"Then that was that. I don't suppose she ever got over it, though."

"Poor Mrs Marrowpip." Churchill was just preparing herself to take a photograph of the snowman's head in the ash bucket when a thought occurred to her. "I don't suppose you were planning to enter your snowman into the Compton Poppleford Christmas Snowman Competition, were you, Mrs Craythorne?"

"As a matter of fact, I was. And now I'll either have to give up or start all over again."

Chapter 7

CHURCHILL AND PEMBERLEY walked through the village in the direction of their office. Oswald trotted on ahead, leaving little paw prints in the snow for them to follow.

"It's interesting that Mrs Craythorne was planning to enter the Compton Poppleford Christmas Snowman Competition, don't you think, Pembers? We could be dealing with an act of sabotage here."

"But how did the culprit know she was planning to enter?"

"Just a lucky guess, I imagine. We could be dealing with someone who wants to win the competition and is therefore destroying everyone else's snowmen."

"How perfectly horrible."

"The attack on Mrs Craythorne's snowman was particularly brutal, wasn't it? Who on earth would go to such lengths as to put a severed head inside an ash bucket? And then knock on the door to summon the householder! There's no doubt the assailant's growing braver with each attack. I know it's not a pleasant case to investigate,

Pembers, but the culprit's revealing something further about themselves with each crime they commit."

"Such as?"

"I haven't exactly determined that yet. But it makes sense, doesn't it? The more crimes this monster commits, the more evidence they're leaving behind."

"I don't even want to catch them," said Pemberley. "Is there really any need? When the thaw comes they won't have any more snowmen to dismember, will they?"

"Perhaps they'll dismember something else."

Pemberley shuddered. "What do you mean by that?"

"I don't know. Garden gnomes, perhaps? I wonder if anyone has ever managed to establish a connection between acts of cruelty toward snowmen and acts of cruelty toward garden gnomes. It wouldn't surprise me."

"I've got a garden gnome myself! He likes to sit next to the birdbath and fish in it. I don't want him coming to any harm!"

"Another good reason to catch this person, Pembers. They shouldn't be allowed to get away with it!"

"If they're only destroying snowmen for the sake of the competition, I hope we won't have anything more to worry about."

"Maybe not. But it's essential we catch them all the same." Churchill's thoughts turned to the more pressing case they were working on. "I think it's about time we learned a little more about our friends from last night's Christmas dinner," she said.

"That's a good idea." Pemberley stopped. "We can start right here."

"Where?"

Pemberley pointed at a shiny blue door with an elabo-rate knocker. A brass plate on the wall next to it read 'Dr Bratchett, General Practitioner.' "He's been a doctor in this village for as long as Dr Sillifant," she explained. "He'll be able to tell us more about him."

"I'm sure there's no need for that."

"Of course there is. You just said yourself that we need to learn more about the other guests."

"We don't need to start with Dr Sillifant, though, do we? Someone more obvious would be a better option."

"Is this because you have a soft spot for him, Mrs Churchill?"

"That's enough about a soft spot! It doesn't exist!" Churchill marched up to the door and tapped the knocker. "Allow me to demonstrate that I'm more than happy to consider him a suspect, Pembers."

The door was opened by a woman dressed in a dark-blue jacket and skirt. Her hair was coiffured into a neat, wavy bob. "Do you have an appointment?" she asked.

"No, I'm afraid not. We're private detectives and we need to question Dr Bratchett about one of his colleagues."

"Dr Bratchett doesn't have time for that. He has a lot of patients to see today."

"We won't take up more than five minutes of his time. It's extremely important, as it relates to the tragic death of Mrs Marrowpip yesterday evening."

"Oh, yes. I heard about that. Has Inspector Mappin given you the authority to question people on his behalf?"

"Erm, yes." Churchill heard the lack of conviction in her voice. "He has indeed," she added a little more firmly.

"Very well. Once Dr Bratchett's finished with his current patient I shall ask him if he has five minutes to speak to you, but I'm afraid it can be no longer than that. And the dog will have to stay outside."

. . .

Dr Bratchett was a small, rotund man who Churchill and Pemberley had encountered when a murder occurred at the vicarage a year previously. A stethoscope hung around his neck and he peered at them through his round glasses.

"I don't know what you want me to help you with," he said as they seated themselves in the chairs at his desk. "I understand Sillifant was present at the tragedy and confirmed the death. There's nothing more I can do. Although he would have had to fetch another doctor to confirm the death. I hope he did that."

"A police doctor turned up," said Churchill.

"That's good, then. Sillifant wouldn't have been able to confirm it on his own."

"Why not?"

"Because he's currently forbidden to practise." He followed this with a smile, suggesting he was rather pleased about it.

"Practise what?"

"Being a general practitioner," clarified Pemberley.

"Oh! You mean he's not allowed to be a doctor? He didn't mention anything about that yesterday evening."

"But he wouldn't, would he?" replied Dr Bratchett. "It's not the sort of thing a doctor would wish to admit to."

"But why isn't he allowed to practise being a doctor?"

"I understand someone made a complaint about him to the Dorset Medical Council. As a result, he's been temporarily suspended from his work."

"He hasn't stopped being a doctor altogether, then? He can practise being a doctor again in the future?"

"If the complaint isn't upheld, yes. He'll be allowed to return to his duties. It's all down to the medical council now, and what they make of it all."

"May I ask what the complaint related to?" asked Churchill.

"No, you may not."

"Oh."

"I'm afraid it's a highly confidential matter. We doctors are used to working in confidence all the time. We're not allowed to tell anybody about anything."

"It must be lovely to know so many secrets."

"Not secrets, Mrs Churchill. It's called professionalism."

"Absolutely. Professionalism. And I can see that you're an extremely professional doctor, Dr Bratchett."

His chest puffed up a little. "Yes, I am. And I'm absolutely run off my feet at the moment, as all of Dr Sillifant's patients have come knocking at my door. They should have thought of that sooner instead of choosing him over me. Now they expect me to just drop my regular patients and make time for them, but I'm afraid my loyalties lie with my own patients. I might squeeze a few of his in if I have the chance."

Dr Bratchett seemed so smug about the position he had found himself in that Churchill hoped she wouldn't be forced to consult him at any point. "I see. Is there anything else you can tell us about Dr Sillifant?"

"I've known the man for many years, but we've never been close. We're rivals, really. I suppose I do feel a bit of sympathy for the chap. After all, someone could easily make a complaint about me and I'd find myself in the same position. But it's more likely that he's done something wrong, and he'll be punished accordingly."

"And what of Mrs Marrowpip?" asked Churchill. "Did you ever meet her?"

"No, she wasn't one of my patients. One of Sillifant's, I imagine."

Pemberley cleared her throat. "If Dr Sillifant wanted to get hold of some poison, how easy would it be?"

"Exceptionally easy. The pharmacist in the village knows us both well, and he just hands the drugs over as soon as we ask for them."

"Interesting," mused Pemberley. "In which case, there are fewer checks and balances in place than if, say, a member of the public were to go in and ask for something?"

"No checks and balances at all. People trust doctors, Miss Pemberley. We're not likely to do anything foolhardy with the drugs, are we? Unless you're suggesting that Silli-fant's the one who poisoned Mrs Marrowpip."

"Can you think of any reason why he might do that?"

"I can't imagine there being any reason at all," replied Churchill.

"I have no idea," said Dr Bratchett, giving Churchill a curious glance in response to her answering a question that had been directed at him. "Now, ladies, I'm afraid that's all I can help you with. I have numerous patients to see."

"Thank you for your time, Dr Bratchett," said Churchill. "We'll be on our way now. Oh, just one further question. I don't suppose you know where Dr Sillifant lives, do you?"

"I do, as it happens. He lives at Coldbone Hall. It's quite a grand place, really. One of his elderly patients left it to him in his will."

"Someone left a large house to him in his will? Well, that's rather generous, isn't it?"

"The patient's family didn't seem to think so when they missed out on their inheritance. But it was quite clear that the patient wanted to leave everything to Dr Sillifant. So there you have it."

"How very interesting," remarked Pemberley.

Chapter 8

THE TWO LADIES and their dog went on their way.

"Isn't it fascinating how some people turn out to be nothing like you imagined them to be?" said Pemberley.

"If you're talking about Dr Sillifant, I'm quite sure he has a sensible explanation for everything, Pembers. Let's not forget that he and Dr Bratchett are rivals, which means we've just had to endure a very biased opinion of the poor man."

"The Dorset Medical Council can't be biased, though. The complaint against Dr Elephant must be serious if they happen to be involved."

"*Silli*fant! I don't ever want to hear you call him elephant again, Pembers."

"Why not? It rhymes."

"And your name rhymes with… Oh, I don't know. It must rhyme with something, but that doesn't mean I should call you it. Anyway, I think it's only fair that we ask the man himself about these dubious-sounding stories. Do you happen to know where Coldbone Hall is, Pembers?"

"On the far side of the duck pond. It was one of the

first houses to be built in Compton Poppleford, so it must be ever so old."

"The one with all the crooked beams that looks as if it's slowly slumping to the ground?"

"That's the one."

When they reached the duck pond, they paused for a moment to watch people skating across the ice.

"Isn't everywhere lovely at Christmastime, Pembers? Snow, ice skaters, halls decked with boughs of holly and the suchlike. Donning our gay apparel and so on."

"I don't have any gay apparel."

"Surely you must have some? You must own a brightly coloured cardigan at the very least."

"All my cardigans are rather dour."

"I thought as much. Perhaps I could knit you one, Pembers. Actually, I won't bother. I never really mastered knitting. Mrs Thonnings could knit you one, though."

"What if Mrs Thonnings is the murderer? I wouldn't want to wear a cardigan knitted by a murderer."

"I can quite understand that; it would put me off, too. Let's wait and see what the outcome of this investigation is before we ask her."

The two elderly detectives continued on to Coldbone Hall.

"I don't suppose we've investigated Mrs Marrowpip's financial situation yet, have we?" said Pemberley. "It would be useful to establish how much property and wealth she left behind, and, perhaps more importantly, who's named in her will."

"That could be very interesting."

"Perhaps Dr Sillifant is named in her will?"

"Oh, here we go again. You're determined to find the man guilty, aren't you?"

"But it happens, doesn't it? The friendly local doctor

befriends a number of wealthy elderly ladies in the hope that they'll leave something nice for him in their wills. If he's very lucky, they might leave him everything."

"That's only happened once to Dr Sillifant."

"How do you know?"

"Because he only needed one home, and here we have it. What a marvellous-looking place." They stopped at the gate and admired the Tudor building's thick oak beams and mullioned windows. "How many rooms does it have, Pembers? It rambles on and on."

"He's built an impressive snowman."

"So he has." A proud-looking snowman in a top hat and bow tie was standing sentry by the neatly cleared garden path. "A sophisticated snowman indeed."

"By the sound of things, Dr Sillifant has a bit of spare time on his hands these days. He's obviously been able to put a lot of effort into it."

"Before we make any more judgments about the man, let's speak to him and hear what he has to say."

A housekeeper in a dark dress answered the door. Churchill introduced herself and Pemberley.

"Dr Sillifant is rather busy, I'm afraid."

"Doing what?" asked the senior detective. "We've just learned that he isn't working at the moment."

"Oh." The housekeeper seemed taken aback that she had been caught out. "I'll go and see if he'd like to talk to you."

To Churchill's relief, she, Pemberley and Oswald were invited inside a few moments later, then escorted to Dr Sillifant's study by the slightly hostile housekeeper.

The study overlooked a snowy orchard, where the fruit trees' ice-encrusted branches sparkled in the sunshine. A fire crackled in the grate and a colourful Christmas tree stood in the far corner of the room.

"How wonderful to see you again, ladies." The doctor's voice was even smoother and richer than Churchill had remembered. "Do please take a seat. I imagine you're quite upset by the events of yesterday evening. I fully understand that. As a doctor, I'm rather accustomed to death, but I realise it can be extremely distressing for those who aren't."

"Thank you for your concern, Doctor," replied Churchill with a broad smile. "It's most welcome."

"The pleasure is all mine."

The housekeeper wheeled in a trolley of tea and cakes.

"Golly, what a pleasant treat," said Churchill. "Something to warm us up a little after all that tramping about in the snow."

"Tramping about in the snow, eh?" The doctor got up and began to pour out the tea. "You're busy with your detective agency, are you?"

"Yes, we're on the trail of a serial snowman smasher."

"A snowman smasher? I've never heard of such a thing."

"Neither had we until a few days ago, but it's been a most distressing case, as I'm sure you can imagine. People put a lot of care into building their snowmen, and then they look outside to see that their masterpieces have been kicked over and decapitated."

"How awful!" Dr Sillifant handed Churchill a cup of tea. "He'd better not go anywhere near Sir Dennis or there'll be hell to pay."

"Sir Dennis?"

"My own snowman creation. I trust you saw him out the front?"

"Yes, he's quite something."

"Isn't he just? I must say that I'm rather proud of

him." He handed Pemberley a cup of tea, then glanced down at Oswald. "Why don't you trot off to the kitchen, little fellow? I've no doubt the cook has a nice juicy bone for you."

"How lovely, Dr Sillifant!" enthused Churchill.

"Oswald doesn't know where the kitchen is," said Pemberley. "And I'm not sure he understood what you said to him just then, Doctor."

"Very well. I'll ask the housekeeper to fetch a bone for him when she returns."

"Thank you, Doctor," said Churchill. "Now, as private detectives we feel compelled to help look into the terrible poisoning of Mrs Marrowpip last night. We're astonished, as no doubt you are, that someone could have got away with putting poison in her plum pudding without the rest of us noticing."

"Absolutely astonishing, as you say, Mrs Churchill. I don't know how the murderer did it! I've been running the evening over and over in my mind, and I still don't understand how it came to pass."

"Mrs Marrowpip was one of your patients, was she not?"

"She was, and I shall miss her very much. Mrs Marrowpip was a regular visitor to my surgery."

"You must be very popular with your patients, Doctor."

He chuckled. "You flatter me, Mrs Churchill, but I do admit that I am rather popular." He adjusted his bow tie. "My patients all seem very grateful for everything I do for them."

"I hear that some of them even give you houses for your efforts."

He sighed. "You haven't been speaking to Dr Bratchett by any chance, have you? He always brings that up whenever my name is mentioned. A touch of green-eyed envy, if you ask me. Yes, I did inherit this wonderful place from a dear old patient of mine. And I'm eternally grateful for it."

"It's a lovely home. Is it just you living here?"

"Just me."

"Oh, that's good."

"And the servants, of course. I wouldn't be without them."

"Naturally." Churchill cleared her throat as she prepared to ask the most difficult question. She put on a smile before asking it. "Dr Bratchett happened to mention that you're not currently allowed to work as a doctor."

"Ah, yes. I expect he very much enjoyed informing you of that. He's quite correct, though. A patient made a complaint about me and, until the Dorset Medical Council realises it was completely false, I'm barred from practising. It's a great inconvenience, as you can imagine, and I miss my patients dreadfully. All I can do now is wait for the ponderous, bureaucratic cogs at the medical council to turn before it eventually acknowledges that a mistake has been made."

"How frustrating, Doctor."

"Such things are sent to try us."

"I'm surprised you didn't mention it to us yesterday evening."

"There wasn't really an opportunity to do so. And it's such a miserable situation to find oneself in that I can't say I was particularly interested in bringing it up and ruining the festive cheer. Besides, it matters very little now, after the sad passing of Mrs Marrowpip. And it's all in the hands of the Dorset Medical Council, who'll soon realise it's a load of nonsense. Can I tempt you to a piece of Christmas cake, Mrs Churchill?"

"How could I possibly resist?"

"Resistance is futile," he chuckled as he cut three large wedges from the fruit cake. "I soaked the fruits in expensive brandy for six weeks."

"Golly! You made this cake yourself?"

"Oh, yes. My favourite part is feeding the Christmas cake. It's had a good dose of brandy every week since I baked it. I enjoyed feeding myself with the leftover brandy too." He grinned.

"I can imagine so, Doctor. What fun."

He handed Churchill and Pemberley a plate each with a thick slice of cake on. "I've always enjoyed baking. I know it's unusual for a professional chap like myself to take pleasure in baking cakes, but I do it all the same."

"Oh, I adore cake," Churchill enthused. "You're a man after my own heart!"

He chuckled. "Am I indeed? That's jolly useful to know."

Churchill bit into her slice of rich fruit cake and savoured the heady warmth of the brandy. "Crikey! It's got quite a kick, Dr Sillifant."

"Oh, good. I aim to please."

The housekeeper peered in to ask if anything else were needed. The doctor asked her to fetch a bone for Oswald.

"Do you have any theories on who might have poisoned Mrs Marrowpip, Doctor?" asked Churchill.

Dr Sillifant sat back in his chair and stroked his neat moustache as he gave this some thought. "Well, she and Mrs Higginbath did exchange some cross words."

"Really? Did you hear what they said?"

"No, but it was while we were playing Hunt the Thimble. Mrs Marrowpip was ferreting about in the writing desk, and I saw Mrs Higginbath stride over to her with a big frown on her face."

"You do realise that's fairly standard for Mrs Higginbath?"

"I know that she's a lady of few charms. But she appeared particularly angry when she spoke with Mrs Marrowpip, and then she immediately strode off again. I thought it was a little uncalled for, given that we were all supposed to be playing a fun parlour game at a Christmas party. There was no need for it in my view."

"Did you see how Mrs Marrowpip responded?"

"She seemed a little dejected afterwards, but that was all. Having said Mrs Higginbath is the only person I suspect at this stage, how she managed to sneak poison into Mrs Marrowpip's plum pudding is anyone's guess. I don't suppose we'll find out unless she confesses."

Chapter 9

"Goodness," said Churchill as they left Coldbone Hall. "Dr Sillifant has strong suspicions about Mrs Higginbath, doesn't he?"

"He's probably trying to deflect attention from himself."

"What do you mean by that, Pembers?"

"If he poisoned Mrs Marrowpip in order to inherit everything she left in her will, he'd want us to suspect Mrs Higginbath instead, wouldn't he?"

"Oh, but that couldn't possibly be true. I simply can't allow myself to believe that the doctor could ever do such a thing! And besides, we don't know if Mrs Marrowpip left anything sizeable in her will yet."

"She owned a successful hardware shop."

"That's true, but shops don't always make as much money as it might appear."

"You're just saying that."

"I am not! Perhaps Mrs Higginbath can tell us more. We'll need to ask her about the cross words she exchanged with her deceased friend, too. Where's Oswald?"

"Behind us somewhere. I can't understand why Dr Sillifant's housekeeper insisted on giving him such a large bone."

The two ladies turned to see the little dog dragging his bone through the snow.

"Oh dear," said Churchill. "It's quite a struggle, isn't it? You'll need to take it off him and carry it, Pembers."

"He won't let me! He gets very angry and snappy whenever I go near it. I can't even work out where a bone that size might have come from. Oh no..." Pemberley paled.

"What is it, Pembers?"

"What if it's a leg bone?"

"It could be a leg bone."

"A *human* leg bone, I mean. A femur or a tibia!"

Churchill shivered. "Surely not! Why on earth would you think that, Pemberley? What's got into you?"

"He's a doctor, isn't he? Perhaps it's from one of his skeletons. Or his patients!" She gave a shudder.

"That's enough, Pembers. Calm yourself! It's quite impossible that Dr Sillifant would have given your dog a human leg bone. You're determined to think ill of the man, aren't you? I don't want to hear any more such nonsense. Now, let's go and speak to Mrs Higginbath so we can get on with our investigation."

Churchill and Pemberley reached the library and waited for Oswald to catch them up.

"At least he has something to keep him occupied," said Churchill as he settled down on the doorstep to chew his bone. "We could probably leave him here all day and he wouldn't even notice."

They headed inside, expecting to see the broad frame

of Mrs Higginbath behind the desk, but in her place sat a lady with golden curls and protruding teeth.

"Mrs Harris?" queried Churchill.

"Hello, ladies!" She gave them a toothy smile.

"Where's Mrs Higginbath?"

"She no longer works here. I'm the librarian now."

"Congratulations on your new position, Mrs Harris. I had no idea Mrs Higginbath had left."

"She has indeed. And she's been banned from every library in Dorset."

"Really?" Churchill felt her jaw drop. "Why on earth has she been banned?"

"For stealing."

Churchill leaned against a bookcase to steady herself. "*Stealing?* Mrs Higginbath? But that's impossible. Surely she would never do such a thing?"

"That's what everyone thought." Mrs Harris shook her head sadly. "Disappointing, isn't it?"

"What did she steal?" asked Pemberley.

"Well, it's all subject to an ongoing investigation." Mrs Harris looked around, as if to ensure that no one else overheard. Then she lowered her voice. "But it seems she was pocketing fines."

"No!" exclaimed Churchill.

"She was overcharging people and pocketing the difference. Let's say, for example, that one of your library books was overdue. The fine for a week is halfpence. Mrs Higginbath was charging a penny and keeping the rest."

"Crikey! It's quite unbelievable," said Churchill. "If she did that all the time she worked here, she must have made a fortune!"

"I think she probably did," said Mrs Harris.

"Why isn't she in jail?"

"Dorset Central Library is still gathering the evidence.

You may be contacted by them at some point, Mrs Churchill, as they're trying to speak to all library users to establish exactly what fines have been paid to Mrs Higginbath over the years."

"I'll be of no use to them," said Churchill. "Mrs Higginbath forbade me from joining the library until recently. It was only after I retrieved her stolen ornament that she finally rewarded me with a reading ticket."

"An eighteenth-century figurine depicting a courting couple," added Pemberley.

"According to the rumours, that's where the money's gone," said Mrs Harris. "On her antique ornament-buying habit."

"She'll just have to sell them to repay everyone, won't she?" said Churchill. "I'm very shocked to discover that she's done something so awful. How did Dorset Central Library find out?"

"A customer complained. Apparently, Mrs Higginbath was seen slipping coins from a fine into her pocket."

"It just goes to show that you can't trust anyone these days, doesn't it?"

"That's right. Anyway, are you looking for anything in particular in the library today, ladies?"

"Only Mrs Higginbath. But we know where to find her now."

The two ladies stepped back out onto the high street.

"It's just as well I have some emergency mince pies in my handbag," said Churchill, opening it up and retrieving a little paper bag. She held it out for Pemberley to take one. "I don't think I'll ever get over the shock of hearing that Mrs Higginbath is a thief."

"It may be a false report," said Pemberley. "I think we

should give Mrs Higginbath the benefit of the doubt for now."

"It's interesting that Mrs Higginbath made no mention of the fact she'd been sacked by the library, isn't it?"

"It's not all that surprising. Just like Dr Sillifant not telling people he's been suspended, I suppose."

"That has to be a false report."

"Perhaps they both are."

"Time will tell, I'm sure. But when people deliberately hide information, it makes you wonder what else they may be hiding."

When they had finished their mince pies, the two ladies made their way to Mrs Higginbath's terraced house. A small, miserable-looking snowman stood in the front garden.

"If she's planning on entering the Compton Poppleford Christmas Snowman Competition, she's got no chance with that one, has she? Oh! Hello, Mrs Higginbath."

The door had been opened before they'd even knocked at it.

"What do *you* want?"

"It's lovely to see you too, this fine morning," replied Churchill. "We'd like to have a quick chat about the events of yesterday evening, if that's all right with you?"

"Go on, then."

Churchill was unsurprised they weren't invited inside. She remained on the doorstep and shivered dramatically to demonstrate how cold it was standing there. "You're no doubt as shocked as we are by the sudden passing of Mrs Marrowpip at Mrs Thonnings's Christmas dinner."

"Yes."

"It's come to our attention that you and Mrs Marrowpip exchanged a cross word or two during a game of Hunt the Thimble."

Mrs Higginbath gave a dry laugh. "Who told you that?"

"We're professional detectives, as you well know, Mrs Higginbath, so we never divulge our sources. As far as we know, it may be untrue. But as we'd heard it suggested, we wanted to give you an opportunity to tell your side of the story."

"Well, Enid Marrowpip was being particularly annoying during that game, as I'm sure you noticed yourself, Mrs Churchill. She was pulling up the carpet and throwing cushions about, and I'd had enough of it."

"We rarely agree on anything, Mrs Higginbath, but I must say I agree with you on that. Were those the only cross words you exchanged?"

"I think so."

"You were good friends, weren't you?"

"Enid, Marigold and I were as thick as thieves at one time," replied the former librarian.

"Marigold?"

"Miss Broadspoon. But then she and Enid became too annoying after a while, so I tried to distance myself from them. As misfortune would have it, Mrs Thonnings invited the three of us to her Christmas dinner party. But don't think I had any reason to put poison in Enid's plum pudding. What would I gain by doing that?"

"I've no idea, Mrs Higginbath."

"I hope I've answered your questions, then. Don't let me keep you from whatever you're planning to do next."

Mrs Higginbath moved to close the door, but Churchill swiftly wedged her boot into the gap.

"I didn't realise you'd been sacked from the library, Mrs Higginbath."

The former librarian glowered at her. "I wasn't *sacked*.

Dorset Central Library asked me to leave while it investigates a complaint against me."

"A complaint about stealing?"

"All completely fabricated."

"By whom?"

"Your guess is as good as mine."

"Well, I'm sure the investigation will reach the right conclusion."

The door was pushed against Churchill's foot.

"Just one more thing, Mrs Higginbath."

"What is it?" came the reply through the gap.

"Was Mrs Marrowpip wealthy?"

"Yes, she was worth a few bob. What of it?"

"Oh, nothing really. Thank you for your help."

Churchill withdrew her boot and the door was firmly closed on the two detectives.

They started walking down the garden path just as Oswald turned up with his bone.

Chapter 10

"I'M GOING to carry Oswald's bone for him," said Churchill. "I can't bear to see him struggling like that."

"I wouldn't, Mrs Churchill…"

Churchill bent down and grasped one end of the bone. She quietly acknowledged to herself that it did resemble a human leg. "Let Auntie Annabel carry this for you, Oswald."

The little dog fixed her with his unforgiving gaze and growled. The bone remained firmly gripped between his teeth.

"I'm not going to steal it. I'm just going to carry it for you so you can keep up with us. You can have it all to yourself once we're back at the office."

Oswald growled again.

"I'm trying to help you."

Churchill attempted to tug the bone from his jaws but soon regretted it. Oswald released his grip on it and jumped at her with such a bout of ferocious yapping that she fell back into a snowy hedge.

"All right!" She held her hands up in defeat. "You can keep it!"

Oswald picked up the bone and Churchill adjusted her hat.

"He's quite attached to it, isn't he, Pembers?"

"Very. And it's all Dr Sillifant's fault."

The two ladies made their way back to the high street.

"Mrs Higginbath said Mrs Marrowpip was worth a few bob," said Pemberley. "I wonder who she's named in her will. Her friendly doctor, perhaps?"

"I'm sure he had no need for her riches."

"Maybe not. But maybe he's just plain greedy."

"He's not greedy, Miss Pemberley."

"You barely know him, Mrs Churchill. How can you be so sure? He does appear to be rather charming and handsome, but they're usually the worst ones."

"Poppycock! Just because someone has a bit of charm, you can't just assume that they're using it to cover up some devious character trait."

"I'm only going by experience."

"You certainly have plenty of that, Pembers, but my instinct tells me Dr Sillifant would never do such a thing."

"Even with his easy access to poison? And the detailed medical knowledge of how much would be required to end someone's life promptly after consuming a mouthful of plum pudding?"

"There are many other lines of enquiry to follow yet. We must keep an open mind. Now, who's this coming our way? Could it be Marigold Broadspoon?"

"Yes, I believe it is."

A myopic woman limped towards them, bundled up in

a thick coat, hat and scarf. "Terrible, isn't it, this snow?" she muttered.

"It's certainly chilly, Miss Broadspoon," said Churchill. "But I do like a bit of snow at Christmastime."

"I don't really see the point of it myself."

"I don't suppose snow has much of a point to it. It's just something the weather does from time to time."

"It's because it rains so much in this country," said Pemberley. "Sometimes it's so cold that the rain freezes and becomes snow."

"You're talking about hail," replied Miss Broadspoon. "I understand hail, but I don't understand snow."

"Perhaps a conversation with a metro... meteor..." began Churchill.

"Meteorologist," clarified Pemberley.

"That's the one," said Churchill. "Perhaps a conversation with one of those would help you understand snow, Miss Broadspoon. How are you holding up, anyway?"

"The hip is still stiff. You probably noticed me limping just then. It feels like it's getting worse, actually. My head has gone from yesterday, though."

"Your head has gone?" queried Pemberley.

"I think Miss Broadspoon is referring to her headache rather than her actual head," explained Churchill.

"Yes, my head has gone, but now it's this..." Miss Broadspoon paused and emitted a loud cough. "That's what I've got now. It's been bothering me since three o'clock this morning."

"Oh dear," responded Churchill, quickly losing sympathy. "A cough can be rather pesky, can't it?"

Miss Broadspoon coughed again. "Yes, it is. I shall have to cover my back and chest in goose fat and brown paper if it carries on."

"It probably doesn't help to be out in this chill air. Perhaps you'd be better indoors beside a warm fire?"

"I shall do that in due course, but I've some groceries to buy first."

"Quite annoying when one has to go out into the cold to buy groceries. And you must be feeling particularly sad today after the passing of your friend, Mrs Marrowpip."

"Yes, I wasn't expecting that. It was all rather sudden, wasn't it? The sooner they arrest Bernard Pouch the better."

"Mr Pouch? Mrs Thonnings's man friend?"

"They're together, are they?"

"Did you not notice?"

"No, I never notice things like that. Come to think of it, I did wonder why he was there. But then it became obvious to me."

"What did?"

"The fact that he was only there to murder Mrs Marrowpip."

"Goodness, Miss Broadspoon – that's quite an accusation! Why would he want to do that?"

"Shopkeeper rivalry."

"A little rivalry is perfectly understandable, but murder would be a little extreme, wouldn't it?"

"Yes it would, but there you go." She followed this with a hacking cough.

"Ugh," said Churchill. "We should let you get on your way, Miss Broadspoon. You don't want to be out in this cold any longer than you absolutely need to be."

Chapter 11

ARRIVING BACK AT THE OFFICE, Churchill took off her snowy boots, coat and hat, and put on her shoes. She warmed her hands by the fireplace and made some tea. A loud thudding noise out on the staircase caught her attention.

"What are you doing out there, Pembers?"

"It's not me; it's Oswald. He's trying to drag that bone up the stairs."

"How very tiresome."

"It's very tiresome indeed. I wish we'd never set foot inside Dr Sillifant's house."

Churchill made herself comfortable at her desk and opened the bag of gingerbread snowmen biscuits she had bought from the bakery. The comforting, spicy smell of ginger wafted up to her nostrils, and her mouth watered as she pulled the first iced snowman from the bag.

"Look out of the window, Pembers," she said.

"I can't," came the reply from the stairwell. "I'm helping Oswald."

"Enormous flakes are coming down now! Isn't it lovely

to be all snug and warm inside when it's so cold and snowy outside?"

Churchill ate her snowman and drank her cup of tea. Then she began to feel a little drowsy.

The next sound she heard was the mellifluent voice of Dr Sillifant. "It's very nice of you to visit me again, Annabel."

"The pleasure's all mine, Jonathan. You have such a beautiful Tudor home."

"Shall we go out into the garden and build a companion for Sir Dennis? I think he'd like a lady friend. A snowlady." He winked.

"What a wonderful idea."

Time skipped forward to the point where they were just putting the finishing touches to their snowy creation.

"She can wear this Christmas bonnet," said the doctor, placing it on the snowlady's head. "Doesn't she look beautiful, Annabel? Almost as beautiful as you." He grinned, and he was just about to embrace her when they were distracted by a movement at the garden gate.

"I'm going to destroy your snowman!" came a shout.

They both turned to see a familiar brown-whiskered figure in a police uniform.

"Inspector Mappin!" she cried out. "You're the serial snowman smasher!"

"Mrs Churchill!"

"Save me from him, Jonathan!"

"Mrs Churchill!"

Inspector Mappin's voice sounded louder and louder, as if he were standing right next to her, and not at the other side of Dr Sillifant's garden at all.

Churchill shook her head and grunted, her eyes flickering open.

She had been asleep at her desk and Inspector Mappin was standing in front of her.

"Did you nod off, Mrs Churchill?"

"No!"

"Your eyes were shut."

"That may be so, but I wasn't asleep." Heat rushed into her face as she recalled her tender moment with Dr Sillifant. "Oh, golly!" She gave her cheeks a gentle slap in an attempt to erase all memory of the dream. "Cripes!"

"Are you all right, Mrs Churchill?"

"Absolutely fine. Never been better. How can I help you, Inspector?"

"I'd like to interview you and Miss Pemberley about the murder of Mrs Marrowpip." He placed his cap on the hatstand and took a seat.

"Make yourself comfortable, Inspector. Miss Pemberley and I will be only too happy to help as witnesses."

Pemberley had taken a seat at her desk and Oswald was lying in front of the fire, chewing his bone.

Inspector Mappin opened his notebook.

"We *are* just being treated as witnesses, aren't we, Inspector?" asked Churchill. "Not as suspects, I hope."

"I'll be the judge of that."

"But we can't possibly be suspects!"

He cleared his throat. "I'll start with the most obvious question. Did you see anyone putting poison into Mrs Marrowpip's plum pudding yesterday evening?"

"No, I didn't. Don't you think I would have stopped them if I had?"

"It may have been a quick, surreptitious movement. Someone reaching over for the salt, for example."

"Salt on a plum pudding?"

"That was just an example. Perhaps brandy sauce would have been a better one. Maybe someone reached across for the brandy sauce and, while doing so, dropped the poison into the pudding."

"That would have been some impressive sleight of hand, Inspector. I don't recall anyone doing that. In fact, I don't think there was any brandy sauce, was there, Miss Pemberley?"

"There was no brandy sauce," her trusty assistant replied.

"I thought not."

"Which was a shame, as I would have liked some."

"Me too! I've just realised we missed out."

'Let's return to the matter at hand," said the inspector. "Did you visit the tea rooms yesterday morning?"

"Yes, we did. We warmed up there after investigating an attack on Mr Pouch's snowman." Churchill's eyes narrowed as she recalled the brief dream in which Inspector Mappin had been revealed as the attacker. *Could there be any truth in that?* she wondered.

"Young boys messing about, no doubt," he replied.

Churchill wondered if this blasé comment was proof that he was trying to deflect their attention from his guilt. "Do you like snowmen, Inspector?"

"I like them very much. And I'm proud to be one of the judges for the Compton Poppleford Christmas Snowman Competition this year. Anyway, we seem to be straying from the topic. You've confirmed that you were at the tea rooms yesterday morning. Did you see Mrs Marrowpip there?"

"As a matter of fact, we did. How did you know that?"

"Witnesses informed me you were there."

"Witnesses? What witnesses? I demand to know who saw us there."

"Everyone I speak to is afforded absolute confidentiality, Mrs Churchill. You know that."

"It's rather perturbing to know that people witnessed us at the tea rooms and were quite happy to tell the police all about it."

"We live in a small village, Mrs Churchill. Nothing much goes unnoticed here. Surely you've realised that by now?"

"I certainly have. I miss the anonymity of life in Richmond-upon-Thames."

"Perhaps you could tell me what your conversation with Mrs Marrowpip was about?"

"It wasn't much of a conversation, we just told her to stop feeding cake to Oswald."

"And then she revealed that she'd seen you feeding cake to Oswald in the past, Mrs Churchill," added Pemberley.

"Yes, thank you, Miss Pemberley. But I don't see how that would be relevant."

"There was a report of angry words being exchanged between yourself, Mrs Churchill, and Mrs Marrowpip," said the inspector.

"Angry words? Not at all!"

"You did get a bit annoyed when she pointed out that she'd seen you feeding Oswald cake," said Pemberley.

"Oh, that. I wasn't annoyed; only very mildly irritated. And I don't remember expressing any angry words whatsoever."

"After Mrs Marrowpip had left the tea rooms, you were heard describing her as an annoying woman," said Inspector Mappin.

"Who on earth told you that?"

"I'm not at liberty to say, as you well know."

"What sort of person sits in the tea rooms listening in to every single word of someone else's conversation, then repeats it verbatim to the local constabulary? I should very much like to know who it was. Who was at the tea rooms yesterday, Miss Pemberley?"

"You don't deny describing Mrs Marrowpip as an annoying woman, Mrs Churchill?" Inspector Mappin probed.

"I can't remember what I said now. But I do remember being annoyed that she had fed cake to Miss Pemberley's dog when he's not allowed to eat cake."

"And you were annoyed that she'd dropped you in it," added Pemberley.

"She *is* an annoying woman. Or rather, I should say *was*. There, I've admitted it, Inspector. But I don't see what all this has to do with anything. Wait a moment… You're not suggesting that I put poison in her plum pudding because she'd annoyed me in the tea rooms, are you?"

Inspector Mappin raised an eyebrow and made more notes in his notebook.

"Inspector," continued Churchill. "You're not considering me as a suspect, are you? I'll admit that my conversation with Mrs Marrowpip yesterday morning was not entirely convivial, but with good reason. And it was the first time I'd ever met her! The second time was in the evening at Mrs Thonnings's Christmas dinner. It's exceptionally sad that she's been poisoned, but I don't know why you feel the need to question me about it."

"I have to question everybody, Mrs Churchill, as you well know."

"I haven't noticed you directing many questions Miss Pemberley's way."

"Miss Pemberley wasn't seen exchanging angry words with Mrs Marrowpip in the tea rooms."

"No, because she always leaves the confrontation to me. She detests conflict."

"I do," agreed Pemberley.

Churchill felt relieved to see Inspector Mappin flip his notebook closed. He didn't ready himself to depart, however.

"Anything else we can help you with, Inspector?"

"Yes, there is one other matter. I don't know if you're aware of this, Mrs Churchill, but Dr Bratchett's secretary, Mrs Piper, is a good friend of my wife's."

"How delightful."

"Mrs Piper happened to mention to Mrs Mappin that you were in there asking questions."

"Yes, that's right. We wanted to find out a little more about Dr Sillifant."

"But your pretext for asking those questions was an assertion that you were helping me with my investigation."

"Golly, Inspector, you used some dreadfully complicated words in that sentence. Have you been reading the dictionary?"

"Stop trying to be clever with me, Mrs Churchill, and answer the question."

"I'm not sure what the question was."

"Did you tell Mrs Piper that you're helping me with my investigation?"

"Those weren't our exact words, were they, Miss Pemberley?"

"No, I don't think so."

"What were your exact words?" asked the inspector.

"I can't remember now. I think we just answered a question she posed to us."

"But the conversation only happened this morning, Mrs Churchill. How is it that you can't remember it now?"

"An awful lot has happened since then, Inspector. And we're both rather upset about the cruel attack on Mrs Craythorne's snowman. The snowman smasher has sunk to new depths."

"I'm going to assume that Mrs Piper reported a correct version of events to my wife. You do know that lying about assisting the police is a serious offence, don't you, Mrs Churchill?"

"Lying about assisting the police? I don't think I've ever done that."

"Good. I hope not. If you had, I could arrest you for it. It's misleading, and it could also affect the course of my investigation. I would have no choice but to describe it as meddling."

"Oh, but we're not meddling, Inspector. We were at that Christmas dinner last night and were very upset, as you can imagine, by the sudden passing of Mrs Marrowpip. It's more than natural for two lady detectives like us to make a few discreet enquiries of our own about the circumstances of Mrs Marrowpip's death."

"I'd rather you didn't."

"We're aware that you're managing the investigation quite capably, and I have every confidence you'll apprehend the culprit forthwith. You needn't worry about us meddling in your case, Inspector. I'll admit we may have meddled in the past, but that's something we try to avoid doing. We're much too professional for that."

"I see that your incident board has already been set up."

"That old thing? It's not really an incident board. It's just a few ideas Miss Pemberley and I were batting about. And actually, they relate to the snowman smasher. We need to find the culprit before the snow thaws."

"Very well. But consider yourself warned, Mrs Churchill."

Chapter 12

CHURCHILL HELPED herself to another gingerbread snowman once the inspector had left. "I think it's quite safe to say, Pembers, that hapless old Mappin has ruined my afternoon."

"He's only doing his job."

"Why are you defending him?"

"I'm not setting out to defend him, I'm merely pointing out that he's doing his job as a police officer. We were at the Christmas dinner party last night when Mrs Marrowpip was poisoned, and witnesses had seen us speaking to her earlier in the day. It's only natural that he would follow up on that lead."

"That's another thing I find annoying. Those witnesses!"

"Every detective needs witnesses, Mrs Churchill. You know that."

"Can you remember who was at the tea rooms at the same time as us?"

"No, I don't, and it doesn't really matter. People have been questioned, and they've reported what they saw. I would do your best to forget all about it, Mrs Churchill. We both know we've done nothing wrong."

"I think we need to pay a visit to Mrs Thonnings, Pembers. Not only should we check she's all right after last night's disastrous dinner, but we should also find out if she has any useful information for us."

"That means we'll have to go out in the snow again."

"What's wrong with that? I thought you liked the snow."

"I do, up to a certain point. But I'm becoming a little fed up with it now. It's so cold and wet. Especially when it melts inside your boots or down the back of your neck."

"We can't let a little bit of weather get in the way of our investigations, Pembers. Come along, now. Let's see what Mrs Thonnings has to say for herself."

It was dusk by the time Churchill and Pemberley called at Mrs Thonnings's home. Large snowflakes spiralled down from the dark clouds and warm lights glimmered in the windows.

"How nice of you to call round," said Mrs Thonnings when she opened the door. "I've been all at sixes and sevens ever since yesterday evening. I haven't been able to open my shop today."

"That's not surprising," said Churchill. "You've had a nasty shock. We've all had a nasty shock, in fact."

Mrs Thonnings showed them into her front room, where Mr Pouch sat on the sofa.

"Good evening, Mr Pouch. Are you here to comfort Mrs Thonnings?"

"Yes, indeed. She needs a lot of comforting."

"As do you, Bernard," said Mrs Thonnings. "You're the one who's had to fire all your staff today."

"Sadly, I have."

"Oh dear," said Churchill. "Did they take it badly?"

"Very badly, yes. They shouted at me and accused me of all sorts of things. It was most unpleasant. And all the while, the poisoning of Mrs Marrowpip has been hanging over us. We can't quite comprehend that it's happened. If someone wanted to do away with her, why couldn't they have chosen a different time of year to do it? Poisoning someone during a Christmas dinner is positively villainous."

"Or perhaps they could have not done it at all," said Churchill. "It's quite a selfish act to murder someone simply because you no longer want them around. The question we need an answer to is: who no longer wanted her around? Do either of you have any ideas?"

Mrs Thonnings shook her head. "None. But I doubt people will miss her, she had many fallings out over the years."

"How long have you known Mrs Marrowpip?" asked Churchill.

"About forty-five years. We always got on well, but I only invited her to the Christmas dinner because I felt sorry for her."

"Why was that?"

"She seemed to have fallen out with all her friends, and I felt that was rather a shame. That's why I invited Mrs Higginbath and Miss Broadspoon, too. I thought the three of them might be encouraged by a bit of Christmas cheer and become good friends again. But instead, it seems one of them has murdered her."

"You think it was Mrs Higginbath or Miss Broadspoon?"

"It can only have been one of them, can't it? It wasn't

me, it wasn't Bernard, and it certainly wasn't either of you two."

"Doctor Sillifant?" ventured Pemberley.

"Doctor Sillifant wouldn't have done it either, Miss Pemberley," said Churchill. "I think Mrs Thonnings is right. We have to look at either Miss Broadspoon or Mrs Higginbath. What are your theories on who might have carried out this vicious act, Mr Pouch?"

"I agree with Gladys. Mrs Higginbath and Miss Broadspoon are the two most likely suspects. I don't think that doctor would have done it. Why would a doctor murder his own patient?"

"Perhaps he persuaded her to change her will and leave all her property and money to him?" suggested Pemberley.

Mr Pouch's eyes widened. "I hadn't thought of that!"

"Doctor Sillifant couldn't possibly have done such a thing," said Churchill.

"But he lives in a house that belonged to one of his patients," said Mrs Thonnings. "I think there could be something in that theory."

"I'm sure there's nothing in it," said Churchill. "Dr Sillifant just doesn't seem the type."

"They never seem the type," commented Mrs Thonnings. "That's the thing."

Churchill steered the conversation back to the former librarian. "We need to establish if Mrs Higginbath sought revenge on Mrs Marrowpip for something, or perhaps she wished to have her silenced."

"Silenced?" said Mrs Thonnings.

"Yes. Did Mrs Marrowpip know something that Mrs Higginbath wanted to keep concealed?"

"That's an interesting theory," said Mrs Thonnings.

"Did you know that she had been fired from the library?" asked Churchill.

"No, I didn't. I knew she had left the library, but I didn't realise she'd been fired. Oh dear... I wonder how that came about. I can understand her not owning up to being dismissed. It's the sort of thing someone could feel quite ashamed about, isn't it?"

"Mrs Harris is the librarian now," said Churchill, "and she told us that Mrs Higginbath had been fired for stealing."

Mrs Thonnings gasped. "*Stealing?* I can't imagine her doing that!"

"It had been going on for some time, apparently, and then someone saw her pocketing part of their library fine. They reported it to Dorset Central Library."

"Gosh! That was brave of them."

"Why do you say that?"

"Because if Mrs Higginbath ever found out who it was, there would be..."

"Wait a moment!" Churchill had a flash of inspiration. "If Mrs Higginbath found out who reported her for stealing from the library, she would have wreaked her revenge, wouldn't she? She possibly would have gone as far as murder!" She turned to her assistant. "Are you thinking what I'm thinking, Miss Pemberley?"

"I don't know."

"What if the person who saw her stealing was Mrs Marrowpip?" said Churchill. "Perhaps Mrs Marrowpip was the one who caused her to be fired?"

Mrs Thonnings gasped again. "Mrs Churchill! I do believe you've solved it!"

Chapter 13

"It's obvious what we need to do today, Pembers," said Churchill as the two ladies arrived at their office the following morning.

"Is it?"

"Yes, it is. We need to visit Dorset Central Library and find out who reported Mrs Higginbath for stealing the money."

"Do you think they'll be willing to tell us that?"

"No, I don't. So we'll need a backup plan."

"Such as?"

"We'll gain access to the written report."

Pemberley groaned. "You know I don't enjoy this type of thing, Mrs Churchill. That means going into places we're forbidden to go, doesn't it? It always gives me the willies."

"But it's necessary, Pembers. Just imagine if we discover that it was Mrs Marrowpip who complained about Mrs Higginbath. Wouldn't it be a wonder to see it confirmed?"

"But Dorset Central Library is in Dorchester."

"That's right, so we'll need to be on our way. I

happened to pass the railway station this morning and have a word with the station master. He told me they've cleared the snow off the tracks, so the branch line is running its normal service."

"Its *slow* service, you mean."

"Exactly. We'll be lucky if we get there by lunchtime."

After a long and tedious train journey, Churchill, Pemberley and Oswald disembarked onto the snowy platform at Dorchester railway station.

"Oi!" came a shout from behind them. They turned to see the train guard pointing at Oswald and shaking his fist. "That dog's not allowed on this train with that bone!"

"But he's just been on the train with that bone," replied Churchill. "For an hour-and-a-half."

"Well, he's not allowed!"

"It's a bit late for that, wouldn't you say?"

He scowled. "Have you bought a return ticket?"

"We have indeed."

"Then he's not allowed to bring that bone on the return journey."

"Very well. You're welcome to try taking it off him on our return journey, train guard. Good luck with that."

Dorset Central Library was a large red-brick building with an inscription that proudly announced it had been opened by the Prince of Wales in 1911.

"This looks like a nice, modern place," said Churchill as they stepped inside. Rows of polished shelving housed thousands of neat, shiny books. "It's so much better than our little tumbledown library in Compton Poppleford. In fact, I'd say that place suffered terribly during the reign of

82

Mrs Higginbath. She didn't exactly keep it up-to-date, did she? She could have learned a thing or two from the librarians here."

"I think I might apply for a reading ticket," said Pemberley.

"Not now, Pembers. We need to concentrate on executing the plan we discussed on the train."

"The first plan is fine, but I don't like the sound of the second one."

"The second plan will only be necessary if the head librarian refuses to tell us who reported Mrs Higginbath."

"Which is highly likely."

"We'll just have to wait and see, Pembers. Perhaps I'll be able to charm him."

"Oh, please don't do that, Mrs Churchill."

"Whyever not? I can be very charming when I need to be. I was well known for it in my youth."

"People make allowances for young, pretty ladies, Mrs Churchill. They don't always make allowances for…"

"*Old* ladies? I realise we're both quite long in the tooth now, Pembers, but being a touch older doesn't mean we've lost all the charm of our younger selves. Let me speak to the head librarian now and see what he has to say for himself."

Churchill asked the young, hook-nosed gentleman behind the desk if she could speak to the head librarian.

"He's very busy," came the reply.

"Aren't we all? I only require a minute of his time."

"May I ask what it's regarding?"

"Yes. It's about Mrs Higginbath, formerly of Compton Poppleford Library."

He raised an eyebrow. "Is that right? In which case, I'll take you to his office."

They were led down a long, wood-panelled corridor to

a door with 'Mr Featherby' written on it. The young man knocked and a strict voice sounded from the other side. "Enter!"

Mr Featherby was a grey-haired, officious looking man with thin lips and a receding chin. His eyes narrowed as he surveyed Churchill and Pemberley. "Who are these ladies, Johnson?"

"It's quite all right. We're able to speak for ourselves," replied Churchill. She introduced herself and Pemberley. "We'd like to speak to you about Mrs Higginbath," she added.

"In what regard?"

"We heard she was dismissed from her post at Compton Poppleford Library."

"That's right. What of it?"

"We're all going to miss her very much."

"That can't be helped, I'm afraid."

"May we ask why she was dismissed?"

"No. That's a confidential matter for library employees only."

"That's a shame. We heard a terrible rumour, and we really don't know if it's true or not. Apparently, she stole money from library funds."

Mr Featherby sniffed and folded his arms. "I can confirm that there was some form of misdemeanour, Mrs Churchill. But it wouldn't do for me to elaborate any further."

"It really is terrible to hear it confirmed. I didn't think Mrs Higginbath had it in her."

"Neither did we. She'd been a trusted librarian for many years. Can I help you with anything else?"

"We're interested to find out how you discovered she'd been stealing."

"There was a witness."

"Was there really? Goodness! And the witness contacted you about what he'd seen?"

"*She*," he corrected. Then he seemed to realise he had given too much away and pressed his lips together, as if to stop himself saying more.

"*She*, is it? How very interesting indeed. I wonder if I know the person who reported her."

"It doesn't matter whether you know her or not, Mrs Churchill. It's all subject to an investigation the Dorset Central Library is carrying out. We shall wait to see if there is any foundation in the allegation once the report is published."

"Does that mean you'll have to prove that she was stealing?"

"Yes, we'll have to prove it. That shouldn't be too difficult, though. We just need to go back through the records. Now, if you'll excuse me, Mrs Churchill and Miss Pemberley, I have work to be getting on with."

"Of course. I don't suppose you'd be interested in sharing the name of the person who reported Mrs Higginbath with us, would you?"

"Absolutely not."

"But it's definitely a she?"

"Possibly a she. Or possibly a he. In fact, I don't even think I can remember at the moment."

"But earlier you corrected me when I said *he*."

"Did I? Well, I don't recall. Anyway, the matter's being dealt with, and it wouldn't do for me to discuss it with anybody outside of Dorset Central Library."

"Nothing could induce you to tell us the name of the person who reported her?"

"Nothing at all!" he leaned forward on his desk. "Did Mrs Higginbath send you here, by any chance? Is she the one who wants to find out the name?"

"No. She doesn't even know we're here. In fact, I shall be frank with you, Mr Featherby. We're not interested in helping Mrs Higginbath. We're curious because this incident may be linked to an investigation we're conducting into the murder of a lady in the village a couple of days ago."

"Really? Well, I'm quite sure that Mrs Higginbath's misdemeanour couldn't have had anything to do with someone being murdered. Now, I really must get on with my work."

"I see." Churchill thanked him for his time, and the two ladies went on their way.

"You know what this means, don't you, Pembers?" said Churchill as the two ladies joined Oswald and his bone on the library steps.

"The *second* plan." Pemberley shuddered. "I hate the second plan."

"It's the only way, and I'm quite confident we can pull it off. You've got the easy bit, and it'll be over quickly for you. I've got the more difficult task."

"And what if we get caught?"

"Let's not think about that now, Pembers. We must focus our energies on the task in hand. Oh! Look at those inviting tea rooms across the road. I suggest we indulge in a little something over there to get our strength back before we embark on our plan."

. . .

After a pot of tea, a round of cucumber sandwiches and several mince pies, Churchill and Pemberley returned to the library.

"Now, you remember what we discussed, don't you, Pembers? Find the section with the largest books. I suspect nonfiction will have the heftiest tomes; all those encyclopaedias and whatnot. They'll be perfect."

"I hope this works."

"How could it not? Just remember to make plenty of noise. That always makes people come running."

The two ladies separated and Churchill began browsing the romance novels, waiting for Pemberley's cue. She was pleased to discover the series of books Mrs Thonnings had lent her in the past. Having read *Forbidden Obsession*, *Reckless Enchantment* and *Clandestine Encounter*, she thumbed through the paperbacks, eagerly looking for the fourth instalment.

"Help! Oh, help!" came a cry from the far end of the library. "I'm trapped under all these encyclopaedias. They fell on me and now I can't..."

A loud crash followed and Churchill held her breath, fervently hoping her assistant was all right. She wanted to go and see but, if she did so, their plan would be ruined.

Shouts of alarm followed, then a flurry of footsteps as people dashed to Pemberley's aid. From her vantage point by the romance novels, Churchill saw Mr Featherby rush out from the corridor and over to the corner where the commotion had come from.

Now was her chance. Churchill estimated she had no longer than five minutes.

She ran as quickly as she could along the corridor to Mr Featherby's office. Fortunately, he'd left the door open in a state of panic.

Churchill scooted over to his desk and began pulling

out the drawers. She found a leaking fountain pen, an ink-stained handkerchief, a library stamp and a packet of Fisherman's Friend lozenges.

Another drawer contained reading tickets that had been cut in half, presumably belonging to those who had been banned from the library. A third drawer contained scraps of paper bearing scrawled lines of poetry, half-finished sentences suggested they had been attempts at compositions.

"Nothing here. Darn it, I'm wasting time!" She dashed over to another set of drawers beneath the window and renewed her rapid search. These drawers were filled with countless brown paper files. They looked like the sort of files which could contain information about dismissed librarians.

Churchill's heart pounded as she searched, every minute spent looking for the information bringing her closer to Mr Featherby's return. Her mouth felt dry.

Footsteps sounded in the corridor. Churchill felt a twinge of panic in her chest. She darted over to the door and hid behind it, praying the head librarian hadn't returned.

The footsteps gradually died away and she managed to start breathing again before rushing back over to the paper files in the drawer.

Her palms felt damp as she leafed through the files. All she needed was the name Mrs Higginbath. Or Compton Poppleford Library. She desperately hoped Pemberley would keep everyone distracted for as long as possible. But there was a limit to how long she would be able to detain Mr Featherby. He could return at any moment.

Eventually she found a file with Mrs Higginbath's name on it. "Thanks be to the Lord!" she whispered, hurriedly opening it up.

More footsteps sounded in the corridor. *Did they belong to Mr Featherby?* She didn't want to waste any more time hiding behind the door now that she was tantalisingly close to finding the information she needed.

Her fingers fumbled as she leafed through the pages. The hairs at the back of her neck prickled as the footsteps grew louder. *Who was it that reported Mrs Higginbath?* The text on the pages seemed to jump around.

The footsteps slowed as they got closer. *It was him,* Churchill felt sure of it. She closed the file and shoved it back into the drawer. Then she tried to shut the drawer, but it stuck. One of the files was in the way. Her heart leapt into her mouth as she tried to adjust it and wedge the drawer closed again, but it was no use. It wouldn't close. She would have to leave it as it was.

Just as Churchill turned to leave, Mr Featherby stepped into the room.

"What on earth?!"

ur
him

sunk

r. Our
ry out a

office? Mr
n answer."

Chapter 14

"WE'VE MET BEFORE, haven't we?" said Chief Inspector Llewellyn-Dalrymple through his thick red moustache. "Mrs Churchill and Miss Pemberley, is that right?"

"That's right."

They sat with Mr Featherby in his office. Pemberley was seated with one foot raised on a chair, a cold compress around her ankle.

"I recall you solving one or two cases down in Compton Poppleford," continued the chief inspector. "You assisted Inspector Mappin, didn't you?"

"I don't believe he's ever formally accepted ~~o~~ assistance, Chief Inspector, but we've certainly helped ~~h~~ solve a few cases."

"You did quite well, as I recall. It's a shame you'v~~e~~ to such depths, Mrs Churchill."

"I haven't sunk to anything, Chief Inspect~~or~~ actions today were entirely necessary for us to ca~~rry~~ vital line of inquiry."

"Snooping about in the head librarian's ~~office~~ Featherby here says you refused to take no for a~~n~~

"He's absolutely right. I simply can't take no for an answer in my line of work, Chief Inspector."

"While I admire your gumption, Mrs Churchill, you can't use it as an excuse to take the law into your own hands. Entering the head librarian's office and going through his personal documents is a trespassing offence."

"Yes, and I'm sorry about that. I didn't think of it as trespassing, but now that you've put it like that, I suppose it is, really. I didn't take anything. I would never do something like that."

"No, but your assistant here has caused a fair bit of damage to some of the books in the library. What's the damage, Mr Featherby?"

"Volume Twenty-Seven of the *Encyclopaedia Britannica*, CHI to ELD, sustained the most damage, sir. Volume Twenty-Eight, ELE to GLA, now has a dented corner. Johnson's having a look at Volume Thirty-Three, STR to ZWO, as we suspect some of the pages may have been folded back on themselves as the book landed on the floor. We've had some strange people in the library over the years, but I've never met anyone before who's pulled a shelf of encyclopaedias onto themselves."

"It looks like Miss Pemberley's paying the price for that now," observed Chief Inspector Llewellyn-Dalrymple. He turned to Churchill. "Was this your idea?"

"I'll admit that we had hatched a plan, Chief Inspector. But Miss Pemberley only intended to create a distraction. She didn't intend to upend the entire shelf! It seems the shelf was much wobblier than she had anticipated."

"But it wouldn't have fallen on her if she hadn't been messing about, trying to create a distraction. Dented encyclopaedias pale into insignificance, however, compared with the act of trespass you've committed, Mrs Churchill."

"Actually, I'd like to dispute that," said Mr Featherby.

"A dented encyclopaedia volume is really quite serious. We pay a lot of money for our encyclopaedias, and our readers quite rightly expect our volumes to be in tip-top condition."

"Which is more serious, then, Featherby?" asked the chief inspector. "A few dented books or the trespass?"

"Erm... The trespass, I suppose."

"Very well."

"But dented books are quite serious, too."

"I get your point." The red moustache bristled and the chief inspector turned back to Churchill. "May I ask exactly what you were looking for?"

"It's quite simple, really. I wanted to find out who had reported Mrs Higginbath for stealing from Compton Poppleford Library."

"She was stealing from the library?"

"That's right."

The chief inspector turned to the head librarian. "Why didn't you inform us of this, Featherby?"

"It's merely an allegation at this stage, sir. We're still in the process of gathering evidence, but if we can prove that wrongdoing has occurred, we will of course bring you in."

"But it's the job of the police to gather evidence. There's no need for you to go taking the law into your own hands."

"I didn't see it as taking the law into my own hands, sir. I viewed it as an internal matter, which the library should be quite capable of dealing with independently of the police."

"It doesn't sound as though you're dealing with it very well."

"I was dealing with it perfectly well until these two turned up."

"Perhaps I might finish explaining what I was looking

for," ventured Churchill. "I wanted to find out the name of the lady who reported Mrs Higginbath, because there has been a horrible murder in Compton Poppleford and we're trying to either prove or disprove Mrs Higginbath's involvement."

"What does Mappin make of it all?" asked Chief Inspector Llewellyn-Dalrymple.

"I have no idea. The inner workings of that man's mind are a mystery to me."

"Same here. I'd better telephone him. May I use your telephone, Featherby?"

"Of course."

The head librarian glared at Churchill and Pemberley as the chief inspector dialled the switchboard and asked to be put through to Compton Poppleford police station.

"Good morning, Mappin," he said after a short pause. "How are things? Good, good. I'm currently in the head librarian's office at Dorset Central Library. You'll never guess who I've got here with me... No, you'll have to try again... Still not right, I'm afraid."

Churchill wondered which names Mappin was putting forward.

"You can save your breath, Mappin, I'll tell you now. It's Mrs Churchill and Miss Pemberley."

There was a pause while Mappin was presumably commenting on the matter.

"Yes, I'm afraid they are. No, not yet. I wanted to ask you about that, actually. Are you looking at Higginbath as a possible suspect?" There was silence while he awaited Mappin's answer. "Why not?" asked the chief inspector. "Mrs Churchill here seems to think Higginbath may have had something to do with poisoning Mrs Marrowpip." Another pause followed. "Evidence?" The chief inspector lowered the receiver from his ear and turned to Churchill.

"Mappin's asking what evidence you've got, Mrs Churchill."

"Well, by accessing the file relating to Mrs Higginbath's dismissal, I've discovered that it was Mrs Marrowpip who reported Mrs Higginbath for stealing from the library."

The chief inspector repeated this information to Inspector Mappin. "We need an arrest. And get on with it!" he added, replacing the receiver.

He turned to the two lady detectives. "On this occasion, Mrs Churchill, you and your colleague, Miss Pemberley, are free to go. It seems you've been of great assistance to the constabulary once again. That looks like a nasty bruised ankle, Miss Pemberley, so I shall ask a constable to drive you back to Compton Poppleford in one of our cars."

"Really?" said Churchill. "That's awfully kind of you, Inspector. Is there space for a small dog with a large bone, too?"

"Is he the one on the step outside? I don't see why not."

"But what about the dented encyclopaedias?" asked Mr Featherby. "And the trespass?"

"We'll sort that in due course. Although, to be honest with you Featherby, I don't fancy doing much paperwork this close to Christmas. Perhaps we can just make a quick note of it and leave it at that?" He turned to Churchill and held up a finger as a warning. "Don't ever let me find you riffling through other people's belongings again, Mrs Churchill. While I have no doubt that your intentions were good, you have undoubtedly committed an offence. Next time the punishment will be quite severe."

"All right, Chief Inspector. You have my word."

Chapter 15

"I DON'T SUPPOSE you've read this article in the *Compton Poppleford Gazette* today, have you?" asked Mrs Thonnings. She waved the newspaper at Churchill and Pemberley, having arrived at their office two minutes after their return.

"No. When would we have had time to read that?" responded Churchill as she helped Pemberley prop her injured ankle up on a chair.

"It still hurts," whimpered Pemberley.

"Of course it still hurts," replied Churchill. "Several volumes of the *Encyclopaedia Britannica* fell on it.

"How did that happen?" asked Mrs Thonnings.

"We'll explain later. For the time being, we need a bit of a breather, Mrs Thonnings. Why don't you read the article from the *Compton Poppleford Gazette* aloud while I make the tea and put some mince pies on a plate?"

"That sounds like a good idea. Here we go." Mrs Thonnings cleared her throat. "'The villagers of Compton Poppleford have been left baffled by a series of attacks on innocent snowmen,'" she began. "'The first took place four days ago. Since then, there have been attacks on Bernard Pouch's and Doreen Craythorne's snowmen.

"'Doreen Craythorne said, "I called on Mrs Churchill and Miss Pemberley because I'd heard good things about their detective agency, but even they haven't managed to catch the culprit yet."'"

"But we only saw her yesterday!" protested Churchill. "How quickly does she expect us to solve it?"

"People are very impatient these days," replied Mrs Thonnings. She continued reading the article aloud. "'Mrs Craythorne added that it should be quite easy to catch the snowman smasher because all the detectives need to do is follow the footsteps back to the person's home.'"

"If she's so sure it's that easy, why doesn't she do it herself? Instead, she's expecting us to do all the work and she's moaning about it."

"It's often the way," replied Mrs Thonnings.

"What else did she say?"

"I think that's all she said. The article goes on to mention that people are becoming too fearful to build snowmen now. There are even a few words from Miss Pemberley here. "'I used to enjoy building snowmen, but having seen the aftermath of these barbaric attacks I'm never going to build one again. It's too risky. I wouldn't want to invite a brutal attack on an innocent lump of snow.'"

"You were quoted in the local newspaper, Pembers!"

"I hadn't realised it was going to be published. Smithy Miggins stopped me on my way home yesterday and asked me about it. Those are pretty much the words I said actually. He's reliably quoted me which is unusual."

"And you didn't feel the urge to comment in your capacity as a private detective investigating these awful attacks? Having heard what Mrs Craythorne said about us, you should have been defending our work, Miss Pemberley!"

"I had no idea she'd said those things! If I had, perhaps I would have said something different. But I thought Smithy Miggins was just stopping for a chat. It never occurred to me that everything I said would be printed." Pemberley's face began to crumple.

"It's all right, Pembers. News reporters are rather unscrupulous, aren't they? Just remember that you can't ever talk to one without it appearing somewhere in print. I'm sorry I was hard on you. I'm a little frustrated by our lack of progress."

Hearing footsteps on the stairs, the three women paused.

A moment later, Inspector Mappin strode in. "Good afternoon, ladies. You'll be relieved to hear that the murderer has been arrested."

"Really?" exclaimed Mrs Thonnings. "That's ever so efficient of you, Inspector. Who is it?"

"Mrs Higginbath."

Mrs Thonnings's face fell. "Mrs Higginbath? I can't imagine her poisoning Enid."

"Well, apparently she did. These things are often a surprise, aren't they?"

"Has she confessed?" queried Churchill.

"No, she's still maintaining her innocence. But Chief Inspector Llewellyn-Dalrymple said she did it, so there we have it."

"Did he actually say that she committed the crime?" probed Churchill.

"Yes. He telephoned me from the library in Dorchester. You were with him, Mrs Churchill, remember? Something to do with some files in the library naming her as the culprit."

Churchill feared Inspector Mappin might have been a little too hasty.

"The library files didn't name her as the *culprit*," she replied. "I just happened to discover that the person who had reported her for stealing was Mrs Marrowpip."

"Yes, that's my understanding, too. That's what the chief inspector told me."

"Mrs Marrowpip reported Mrs Higginbath for stealing?" queried Mrs Thonnings. "Oh dear! Enid always was a stickler for these things. Mrs Higginbath can't possibly be a murderer, though. I don't believe it."

"We've uncovered a motive for Mrs Higginbath," said Churchill, "but that doesn't mean she poisoned Mrs Marrowpip."

"Well, that's what the Chief Inspector said, and he was following your advice, Mrs Churchill," replied Inspector Mappin.

"Are you sure the chief inspector told you Mrs Higginbath was the culprit?"

The inspector frowned. "I don't remember his exact words now. I was merely acting on what I understood his words to have been."

"Perhaps you need to clarify with him exactly what he said?"

"Where's the evidence?" asked Mrs Thonnings.

Inspector Mappin frowned again. "I just assumed, from the manner in which the chief inspector spoke, that there must be evidence. Where's the evidence, Mrs Churchill?"

"There's no firm evidence yet. It's all circumstantial. Anyway, Mrs Higginbath clearly had a motive, but did she have the means?"

"I don't know," said the inspector. "Did she?"

"That's what we need to find out. Maybe Mrs Higginbath took the poison with her to the party? I suppose you could find that out by examining her handbag."

"I never look inside a lady's handbag, Mrs Churchill."

"But you absolutely must on occasions like this, Inspector. In fact, you'll need to have a poisons expert to look inside her bag. If she used it to transport the poison, I'm sure traces would have been left."

"Absolutely. I was planning to do that, of course."

"What if no traces of poison are found inside her handbag?" asked Mrs Thonnings. "Does that mean she's innocent?"

"Not exactly," replied the inspector. "But now I come to think of it, perhaps the chief inspector didn't tell me outright that Mrs Higginbath was the culprit. Perhaps I was just a little excited to have received a telephone call from him."

"Where's Mrs Higginbath now?" asked Mrs Thonnings. "Please don't tell me you've locked her up in a police cell!"

"That's where people go when they're arrested," replied the inspector.

"But you're going to let her out soon, aren't you?"

"We'll have to examine the handbag for traces of poison first, then go from there. But if this turns out to be an enormous mistake, we'll all know where the fault lies." He glared at Churchill.

"And why would it be my fault, Inspector?"

"Because you're meddling again, Mrs Churchill. I don't know why you took it upon yourself to break into the head librarian's office..."

"I didn't break in. It was already open."

"Well, it sounds as if you were sticking your nose in

where it shouldn't have been, Mrs Churchill. And if I'm mistaken about Mrs Higginbath, and the chief inspector is also mistaken, it's going to be very embarrassing indeed for both of us." He placed his hat back on his head. "I came here to thank you, Mrs Churchill, but now a seed of doubt has been sown in my mind."

"I'm afraid that's detective work for you, Inspector."

"So it seems. I won't be happy if it turns out I'm mistaken." He wagged a finger as he headed out of the door. "My advice, Mrs Churchill, would be to stick with snowmen."

Mrs Thonnings wiped her eyes. "Poor Mrs Higginbath. She may have stolen from the library, but she doesn't deserve to be locked up in a police cell."

"I think it's a very suitable punishment for her if she'd been stealing from the library," said Pemberley. "They should have involved the police from the outset."

"But it's not fair that they've accused her of murder. She would never do such a thing!"

"To my mind, Mrs Thonnings, none of the guests at your Christmas dinner seemed likely to have done such a thing," said Churchill, "but it turns out that one of them did, and that's the challenge facing us. Now then, we have a few tasks at hand. Not only do we have to solve the case but we also need to stop people moaning about us in the local newspaper. We'll get hold of that snowman smasher and restore our reputations."

"How?" asked Pemberley.

"We lure them in."

"How?" asked Mrs Thonnings.

"We provide bait."

"Bait? Mealworms or something?"

"No! A snowman. We need to build the biggest and best snowman ever seen. A snowman so impressive that it will entice the smasher to destroy it. All we need to do is build it, then lie in wait to see who comes along to smash it up."

Chapter 16

"WE'LL BUILD the snowman in your garden, Miss Pemberley," said Churchill as they pulled on their boots, overcoats, hats and scarves. "You live in the centre of the village and the snowman will be easy for the culprit to spot. My cottage is a bit out of the way."

"But my ankle hurts."

"I think you're using that as an excuse."

"A little bit."

"I'll help you walk there; you can put your arm around my shoulders. If it's still unbearable when we get there you can rest by the fire for a while."

"Would you like me to help?" asked Mrs Thonnings.

"Absolutely," replied Churchill. "All hands on deck!"

The three ladies slowly made their way to Pemberley's cottage. It sat on a snowy little lane where smoke curled up from chimney pots and a robin eyed them from its perch on a snow-filled window box.

Churchill surveyed the scene. "You don't have much of a front garden, do you, Miss Pemberley?"

"No, I don't. We'd be better off building it in the back garden."

"But we need to build it out the front, where the snowman smasher can see it."

"All right, then."

Mrs Thonnings had already piled up some snow and was rolling it along the lane to create a large ball.

"That's the ticket, Mrs Thonnings," said Churchill. "Efficient as always. We haven't long until sunset now, so we'd better get a move on."

The three ladies spent the next hour building the snowman. Once they had finished, they stepped back to admire their creation.

"He's a little wonky," said Mrs Thonnings.

"And quite fat," added Pemberley.

"What's wrong with either of those things?" asked Churchill. "They give him character. All we need now is a carrot for his nose."

"I don't have any carrots," replied Pemberley.

"You don't have any carrots? Everybody has carrots!"

"I don't. I've never liked them."

"Parsnips?"

"I don't like them either."

"What have you got that we could use for his nose?"

"A potato?"

"That will have to do, I suppose."

"Nothing wrong with a potato," said Mrs Thonnings. "Mrs Rumbold's got a nose like a potato."

Churchill nodded. "Now you come to mention it, she has. Perhaps you could pop indoors, Miss Pemberley, to see what else you can find to give our snowman a bit of personality."

Pemberley did so. She returned a short while later with a curious collection of items. "Here's the potato."

"That's enormous!" said Churchill.

"It's all I have. And I've got these raisins for the eyes."

"So he'll have an enormous nose and tiny eyes?"

"Just like Mrs Rumbold," said Mrs Thonnings. "It's almost uncanny."

"I thought we could use these tiddlywinks for buttons," said Pemberley. "I found them in a drawer in my side-board. Look, they're quite colourful, aren't they?"

"Very well, put the colourful tiddlywinks on him. What else do we have?"

"I don't have a scarf we can use, but I've got this red feather boa."

"A feather boa? Very fancy! I didn't have you down as the feather boa type."

"I kept it from my days as a companion to a lady of international travel. It was just a little something I bought to liven up my outfits when we frequented the nightclubs of Berlin."

"Golly. Now, please tell me you have a hat, Pembers."

"Yes, this Easter bonnet."

"Not a Christmas bonnet?"

"No, I don't have one of those."

"A Christmas bonnet would have looked very nice on our snowman," said Churchill, "but seeing as time is of the essence, we'll have to go with the Easter bonnet for now."

She watched as Pemberley placed the straw bonnet on the snowman's head, complete with paper daffodils and papier mâché Easter eggs.

"There." Churchill stepped back to admire the snow-man. "I think he looks rather interesting."

"And a pipe," said Pemberley, pushing an old wooden pipe in just below the potato.

"Intriguing. He's certainly very eye-catching."

"Oi!" came a voice from behind them.

They turned to see a small man leaning on a stick.

"Hello, Mr Groggins," said Pemberley. "How are you?"

"You've stolen all my snow." He pointed his stick at the exposed cobbles outside his cottage.

"You mean we've cleared a slippery hazard from in front of your home, Mr Groggins," said Churchill. "I'd say we've done you a service."

"And what if I want to build a snowman for the Compton Poppleford Christmas Snowman Competition? How would I do that? There's no snow left. You've taken it all!"

"Can't you borrow some from over there?" Churchill asked, pointing to the other side of the lane.

"No, that's Mr and Mrs Burnage's snow. They don't want me ransacking their snow to build a snowman. What if they want to build one? They'd have to take some snow from outside Mrs Foyle's cottage. And what if she wants to make a snowman? Do you see my point? You can only build a snowman with the snow you've got outside your own house."

"I didn't realise there were rules regarding the owner-ship of snow outside one's home," replied Churchill. "As far as I can see, it's fallen freely from the sky and belongs to us all."

"It's not that simple, Mrs Churchill. It's a matter of sharing resources, don't you see? If someone's greedy and uses up all the snow, there's less left for the rest of us!"

Churchill agreed to some extent. Although the old man was being petty, she wasn't sure how to argue with him any further. "Perhaps you'd like to share our snowman?"

He sneered. "Looks like a snow*lady* to me, what with that feminine bonnet."

"Does it matter whether it's a snowman or a snowlady?"

"I'd prefer a snowman."

"It *is* a snowman," said Pemberley. "A snowman who enjoys wearing Easter bonnets."

Mr Groggins shook his head in dismay. "Well, it wouldn't surprise me if your snowperson gets knocked down, anyway. That's what's been happening around here lately, isn't it?"

"That's the intention," said Mrs Thonnings.

"Shush!" said Churchill. She glared at the red-haired haberdasher, not wanting her to reveal any more of their secret plan. Then she turned to Mr Groggins. "We'll do you a deal. If this snowman gets knocked down, you can have all of his snow for yourself. Does that sound fair?"

"It does, actually," he replied. "Thank you." Then he stepped back inside and closed his door.

"Now what do we do?" asked Pemberley.

"We lie in wait, Pembers. We sit in your kitchen and peer out through this window here."

"But we'll be seen!"

"Not if we keep the lights off and peer through a tiny gap in the curtains. Then, when we see someone sneak up, ready to destroy our snowman... we *pounce*!"

Chapter 17

MRS THONNINGS WENT on her way and Churchill and Pemberley seated themselves by the window in Pemberley's kitchen. It was almost dark outside but the snowman was well lit by a nearby lamppost.

"This view is perfect, Pembers. The snowman smasher doesn't stand a chance of getting away with it now."

"We need to pull the curtain across and peek out through a gap at the side, Mrs Churchill. Otherwise, he'll be frightened away by your face."

"I beg your pardon?"

"I didn't mean to suggest that your face is frightening; I just meant that the mere sight of it would undoubtedly deter him."

"You're not making it sound any better, Pembers."

Pemberley pulled the curtain across, and the two ladies took up their positions on either side of the window.

"Isn't this exciting?" said Churchill. "I do enjoy setting a trap for someone. The suspense is quite thrilling, isn't it? I wonder who the snowman smasher will turn out to be." Despite her state of exhilaration, Churchill was already starting to feel uncomfortable on her wooden chair. "Do you have any mince pies, Pembers?"

"I do, but I'm keeping them back until later."

"Why not now?"

"Well, we may be in for the long haul. I thought the mince pies could be something for us to look forward to."

"I think we should have one now, just to get us going. Then we can have another one a bit later when we feel our energy levels beginning to flag."

"Very well, Mrs Churchill, but we need to make sure we don't run out, because we have no idea how long we're going to be sitting here."

"What's the time?"

"I don't know. I can't see the kitchen clock because it's too dark, but I think it must be about half-past four."

"Is that all? Winter evenings are so long, aren't they?" She recalled how the snowman smasher had called at Mrs Craythorne's home at nine in the evening. "We could be here for another five hours."

"At least."

"I'm beginning to wish we'd planned this a little better, Pembers."

"I'd say we've planned it rather well."

"I mean in terms of sustenance. If all we've got to keep us going are a few measly mince pies, I'll be on my knees by the end of the evening."

"My mince pies aren't measly!"

"I didn't quite mean it like that, Pembers; I'm sure they're lovely mince pies. What I meant was, they're not enough to sustain us. I should have organised more provisions."

"For all we know, Mrs Churchill, the attacker may strike half an hour from now. Then we'll have caught them and our job for the evening will be done."

"That would be marvellous." Churchill desperately hoped it would be the case.

An hour later, the two ladies sombrely helped themselves to a mince pie from the tin. Oswald was enjoying a hearty meal of boiled tripe and Churchill felt tempted to steal some for herself. She tried to ignore the rumble in her stomach and continued to peer through the gap in the curtains. "There's nothing much going on out there is there?"

"No, it's a very quiet lane," Pemberley replied. "Hardly anything ever happens around here."

"Do you have anything to drink?"

"Water?"

"Water? How could water possibly sustain me on an evening like this? I was thinking about something a little stronger."

"A cup of tea?"

"If it were four o'clock in the afternoon, I would take you up on that offer, but I feel the need for something much stronger now."

"Brandy?"

"That's more like it! A brandy would do me very well indeed. Thank you, Pembers."

Churchill kept watch while Pemberley made the drinks. She could hear her trusty assistant bumping and crashing her way around the kitchen.

"Why don't you put a light on, Pembers?"

"I can't. The snowman smasher will see us."

"Surely it would be all right for just a few minutes?"

"I don't think it would."

Churchill sighed. "In hindsight, we should have set up a little food and drinks table while we still had the lights on.

That way we could have helped ourselves whenever we needed a little something. Perhaps even a food and drinks trolley like the one Dr Sillifant has. That may be something to bear in mind for the next time we do this."

"We don't have to do this again, do we?"

"Who knows? But at least if we do, we know how to prepare ourselves."

The two ladies heard the church bells chime six as they sipped their brandy.

"Very useful, aren't they, church bells," commented Churchill. "They tell you what time it is even on occasions when you can't look at a clock."

"They've been useful for hundreds of years," agreed Pemberley. "They used to tell the peasants when to go out into the fields and when to come back in again."

"Can you imagine working in a field all day, every day, Pembers? That's what your forebears used to do."

"And your forebears, Mrs Churchill."

"Oh, no. I don't think so. I'm sure my forebears lived in the manor house. I'm quite certain there's some aristocratic lineage in my family."

"What makes you say that?"

"I've explained the Churchill connection before, haven't I? There's undoubtedly a link to the Duke of Marlborough in there somewhere."

"But that's your married name."

"Yes, that's true. But there must have been some landed gentry on my mother's side. You can see it in the nose."

"*Inside* the nose?"

"No, just in the shape of the nose. It has a refined shape."

"Didn't peasants ever have refined noses?"

"I doubt it. They probably had peculiar noses like the one on our snowman. It's reasonably easy to look at someone these days and ascertain whether they're descended from the peasantry or the aristocracy."

"If you're descended from aristocracy, Mrs Churchill, why did you marry a policeman?"

"Well, the trouble with the aristocracy is that everything gets left to the eldest son. I'm probably descended from a seventh-born daughter or something similar. In that case you inherit nothing other than good breeding. I also have my suspicions that the money in my family was gambled away by some errant earl, as was so often the case in those days."

"Oh! I think I saw some movement out there!" whispered Pemberley.

The two ladies stared out into the snowy scene, lit by the solitary lamppost.

"Ah, it's just a cat," commented Pemberley. "Probably Mr Groggins's."

"That's a shame. I thought it might finally be our assailant." Churchill picked up her glass and realised it was empty. "How many brandies have we had?"

"Two."

"Do you think there's any possibility of having another?"

"I'll have to see how much is left in the bottle."

By the time the church bell chimed eight, Churchill was struggling to focus on the view outside. "I don't think the culprit's heading this way tonight. They're probably busy toppling snowmen over on the other side of the village as we speak."

"It's only just gone eight, Mrs Churchill. They could be here any minute."

"My posterior's numb." Churchill got to her feet and stomped about in an attempt to get some sensation back.

"The snowman smasher might hear you!"

"They're over on the other side of the village, Pembers! Besides, I have to restore the blood flow to certain parts of my body or the results could be quite disastrous. Have we finished all the brandy?"

"Yes."

"And the mince pies?"

"Yes."

"Oh dear."

"There might be some bread."

"I don't want bread, Pembers. Not after those lovely mince pies. Bread would be so disappointing. Anything else to drink?"

"All I've got is some elderflower wine."

"Not my favourite wine."

"Nor mine, But I do have some mulling spices, so maybe we could mull it and see if that helps."

"What an excellent idea, Pembers. You mull the elderflower wine while I mull the case over by the window."

Pemberley clattered about in the kitchen, knocking things over and accidentally catching a finger on something hot.

Eventually, Churchill found herself with a glass of warm, mulled elderflower wine in her hand.

"Cheers, Pembers. Down the hatch."

"Cheers, Mrs Churchill. Oh, what's that on the window?"

"While you were mulling the wine, I breathed on the glass and drew a little nativity scene in the condensation with my finger. Do you like it? There's little baby Jesus in the manger, and there's Mary and Joseph. I've just started on the animals. I'm not sure if that one's a cow or a sheep, but it doesn't really matter, does it? You get the idea that there are some animals in there with them. They've got four legs, and that's all that matters. I was just about to move on to the shepherds when you put this rather lovely glass into my hand. How many shepherds do you think there were?"

"You may have scared away the snowman smasher, Mrs Churchill! Perhaps they walked up to the snowman, saw your finger drawing on the window and ran off!"

"I didn't see anybody outside."

"That's probably because you were concentrating too hard on your nativity scene. I hope you didn't scare the snowman smasher away."

"If I did, it would suggest that we're dealing with a scaredy cat, wouldn't it?"

"I think it's fairly obvious that we are. Anybody who goes around knocking down snowmen at night has to be a coward."

"I agree, it's a very cowardly thing to do. I haven't seen any carol singers passing by this evening. You'd have thought they'd have come this way, wouldn't you? We need a little something to keep ourselves entertained. I suppose I shall have to provide some yuletide carols myself."

"I don't think that's a good idea."

Churchill cleared her throat. "'Tis the season to be jolly,'" she warbled.

"Please don't sing, Mrs Churchill."

"My glass appears to be empty, Pembers. How did that happen? Do you know what I've always wanted to do? Dash through the snow in a one-horse open sleigh. Wouldn't that be fun? I don't know anybody with an open sleigh I could borrow. Farmer Drumhead's got a few horses, and I reckon he'd probably lend me one. Where do you suppose I could buy one of those sleighs? I imagine it would be rather pricey, and I'd only really get any use out of it a few days each year. A week or two at most. It would be difficult to get my money's worth. But perhaps it's worth it, just to go dashing through the snow. Bells on bobtails ring! Oh, goodness. If I didn't know better, Pembers, I'd say that I was a little squiffy."

Chapter 18

THE KITCHEN WAS FILLED with a pale grey light when Churchill awoke. She had fallen asleep, slumped over in her chair. "Oh, good heavens!" she said with a start, feeling a pain in her neck from the awkward angle she had slept in. Her right hand had been holding an empty glass that had toppled over, leaving a damp patch on her skirt. "Oh, no. Harris Tweed doesn't cope well with mulled wine dregs. Oh dear, oh dear. What happened?" She glanced over at the other chair, where Pemberley dozed with Oswald curled up on her lap.

"Oh, my head…" Churchill rubbed at her temples. "My mouth feels like the Sinai desert. Pembers, wake up!"

Oswald stirred and briefly looked up at Churchill before nestling his nose behind his paw, giving a lazy sigh and preparing to doze off again.

"Pembers!" Churchill leaned forward and gave her assistant a gentle shake. "Wake up! We fell asleep!"

Pemberley stirred. "What's happened? Where are my glasses?"

"Here they are." Churchill bent forward and picked

them up from the kitchen floor. Every muscle and bone in her body ached from her night in the wooden chair.

"Our snowman!" exclaimed Pemberley. "Is he still there?"

Churchill pulled open the curtains and looked out. The rising sun cast a warm glow over the snowy rooftops. She pressed her nose against the windowpane and all she could see in place of their snowman was a mound of snow. "Oh, no!"

Pemberley lifted Oswald down from her lap and got to her feet before cautiously peering out of the window. "Don't say that he's..."

"Gone!" replied Churchill with a lump in her throat. Then her fists balled with anger. "And we missed the smasher! They must have snuck up the lane while we were asleep! Just wait till I get my hands on that little..."

"How do you know they're little?"

"I don't. I didn't really know what to call them. Frankly, Pemberley, I'm lost for words. How could they do such a thing?"

"How did we miss them?"

"We fell asleep. It was all that wine you kept giving us."

"You asked for the wine, Mrs Churchill. I would have been happy with a mince pie or two, but you demanded brandy and mulled wine."

"We would have fallen asleep even earlier without it. Let's go outside and survey the damage."

"Must we?" Pemberley's voice cracked with emotion.

"I realise it won't be easy, Pembers, but we must be brave. Stiff upper lip and all that."

They went out into the lane and surveyed the sorrowful snowy heap.

Mr Groggins joined them, leaning on his stick. "Oh dear. Looks like he's struck again."

"Where's the Easter bonnet?" asked Pemberley, looking around.

Churchill bent down and retrieved the tiddlywinks, potato, pipe and feather boa, but there was no sign of the bonnet. "The smasher has obviously taken a shine to it and kept it as a trophy."

"But that was my favourite Easter bonnet!" wailed Pemberley.

"If it was your favourite bonnet, Pembers, why did you put it on a snowman? You knew there was a chance that this might happen."

"But I didn't expect them to take my Easter bonnet! It's Christmastime!"

"That's right, it's Christmastime. That just goes to show how cruel and hard-hearted this sorry individual is."

"Look what's appeared on my gatepost," said Mr Groggins, pointing at it with his stick.

Churchill turned to see and gave a shudder as the snowman's raisin eyes stared out at her from the head on the post. "Chilling," she said.

Although the snowman had been purposefully built as bait, Churchill finally understood the sadness of the others whose snowmen had been destroyed. "The snow's all yours now, Mr Groggins," she said. "I hope you enjoy it."

After a breakfast of eggs, bacon, thickly buttered toast, and several cups of tea, Churchill found herself in a more determined mood. "Although it's highly regrettable that we missed the snowman smasher last night, Pembers, all is not lost. Their footprints have been perfectly preserved in the snow."

"Yes! We can just follow the tracks to their house!"

"Exactly."

"So our snowman smasher trap worked after all."

"Potentially. Let's see where the footprints lead us first."

The two ladies wrapped up warm and set out into the bright morning sunshine.

"It's the same footprint we saw at the other crimes, isn't it?" commented Churchill as they examined the scene. "Here they are leading up to the snowman, and there they are leading away again. All we need to do now is follow them."

They marched on, following the footprints with Oswald happily trotting ahead.

"Thank goodness he's forgotten about that bone today, Pembers."

The little dog paused and glanced back at them, as if he understood what Churchill had said.

"Shush! Don't remind him."

They reached the end of the lane where the trail forked. "Here we have a dilemma," said Churchill. "The set of prints leading to the scene has come from the right. However, the trail of footprints leaving the scene bears to the left. It appears that the assailant approached and left by different routes. That's a shame. I'd hoped that both trails would have led us straight to their house."

"Right goes in the direction of the duck pond and left leads towards the high street," said Pemberley.

"I'll go right and you go left, Pembers. We've nearly got them, I feel sure of it."

The two ladies separated and Oswald trotted after Pemberley. Churchill hoped the footprints she was following would lead directly to an address, but she soon discovered, to her great disappointment, that they led her on a roundabout route up and down a series of little lanes.

On Honeysuckle Lane, she discovered another

snowman had been knocked to the ground. A woman and two sad-looking children were carefully rebuilding it.

"We only made our snowman yesterday, and we discovered this morning that the snowman smasher had struck," said the mother.

Churchill was hit with a pang of sadness. "How awful!"

"I'd read about the smasher in the newspaper, but I didn't think they would sink so low as to destroy a snowman built by children."

"They're utterly heartless." Churchill shook her head. "That's two snowmen they've destroyed in one night, and there may be others, too. I'm following this trail of footprints in the hope that they'll lead me to their door. Leave it with me. I'm determined to find them!"

"Thank you," replied the mother. "They need to be brought to justice. Can the police actually arrest them for it, though?"

"Oh, I'm sure they can."

"On what grounds?"

Churchill gave this some thought. "That's a good question. Wanton destruction?"

"Is that a real offence?"

"I'm positive it is. Or vandalism, perhaps. Oh, and I've just thought of another one. Trespass. That would be a good one."

"Yes, I suppose that could work. Although how they're going to prove who did it, I really don't know."

Churchill went on her way, following the footprints. She turned left, then right, then went back on herself a bit before turning around, leading off to the right, heading through an alley and emerging out onto the high street. Here the footprints criss-crossed with countless others, but Churchill did her best to follow the trail. After losing the prints for a moment she found them again, and quickly discovered they led up to the Wagon and Carrot public house.

Pemberley and Oswald stood outside it.

"Oh dear, Pembers. A dead end for you, too?"

"It looks like they came out of the Wagon and Carrot, then returned to it again," said Pemberley. "That doesn't exactly narrow things down, does it?"

"We'll have to ask the landlord who was in here yesterday evening."

"It gets very busy in the evenings. That's one of the reasons Mrs Thonnings and I stopped going."

"I didn't know the two of you had been meeting regularly at the pub."

"We've stopped now."

Churchill sighed. "This is all terribly frustrating. Just when we thought we were on their tail, the trail goes cold."

"I see Mrs Higginbath heading our way."

"That's all we need. That means she must have been released. Let's make a move."

The two ladies attempted to hurry away, but it was too late. "Hold it right there!" commanded the former librarian.

"Oh, Mrs Higginbath!" said Churchill as sweetly as she knew how. "This is a pleasant surprise. How are you this fine morning?"

"Tired."

"I know the feeling."

"I was arrested!"

"Oh yes, I think we heard something about that."

"You *think* you heard about it? I was told it was you who ordered that I be arrested."

"Oh dear. Inspector Mappin is so very unreliable in the way he relays information. I didn't ask for you to be arrested at all, Mrs Higginbath. I merely discovered an interesting link between you and Mrs Marrowpip."

"What sort of link?"

"I discovered that she was the one who reported you to Dorset Central Library for stealing."

"It was *you* who discovered that? Inspector Mappin told me Enid was the person who'd reported me after he arrested me yesterday. I suppose you like to think you're being very useful when you're carrying out your so-called detective work, Mrs Churchill, but you're merely complicating matters. Thanks to you, I've just spent a night in the police cells for absolutely no reason at all!"

"You didn't know it was Mrs Marrowpip who had reported you?"

"No! The head librarian refused to reveal the identity of the person who had been telling tales. I had to wait until I was arrested before I could find out. The shame of it! It took me some time to convince Inspector Mappin, but he eventually realised I had no reason to poison Enid."

"I must say I didn't expect Inspector Mappin to act so swiftly on the information. It seems he can be rather heavy-handed with his handcuffs."

"Well, at least I'm in the clear now. Which is more than can be said for you, Mrs Churchill."

"What do you mean? I'm in the clear, too. What motive could I possibly have for poisoning Mrs Marrowpip?"

"Your argument with her at the tea rooms. There were many witnesses, I believe. I'm off the hook, but you'd better watch your back, Mrs Churchill!"

Chapter 19

"THE CHEEK OF IT!" exclaimed Churchill once Mrs Higginbath had walked away. "What does she mean by telling me to watch my back?"

"Just ignore her," replied Pemberley. "She's only bitter because she was arrested and everybody knows she stole from the library. She's got nothing left to lose now, so she obviously feels the need to march about being horrible to people."

"I think you may be right there, Pembers. Although she was marching about being horrible to people before any of this happened. Never mind. Shall we go and enjoy something restorative at the tea rooms? I feel the need for a nice, warm sit-down."

The two ladies and their dog made themselves comfortable at a table by the window. They ordered two large Christmas fancies and a pot of tea.

Churchill glanced around the room. "Just think, Pembers, the witnesses who claimed to have seen me exchanging angry words with Mrs Marrowpip could be right here. Do you recognise any of them?"

"I recognise most of the people in here, but I can't recall who was here when we encountered Mrs Marrowpip."

"Isn't it vexing? I'd like to have a word with whoever it was."

"I'm sure there's no need, Mrs Churchill. The witnesses would only have reported what they thought they saw. It's time to forget about it and concentrate on the other conundrums we're dealing with."

"They certainly are conundrums, aren't they? Who is the snowman smasher and who is the plum pudding poisoner? Could they be the same person?"

"If it is, they're having a busy Christmas."

"And making it rather busy for us, too. It would be nice to have everything wrapped up in time for Christmas Day, wouldn't it? That's only three days away now. Oh, look! Miss Broadspoon's here. But who's that young gentleman sitting with her?"

Pemberley glanced over at their table. "I don't know."

The young man had wavy brown hair, a large nose and thick-lensed spectacles.

"I tell you what, Pembers, you can see the family resemblance between them."

"I didn't think Miss Broadspoon had any family."

"Everybody has family, Pembers."

"I assumed she had parents, but I've never heard of her having any other relatives."

"Well, I would venture to say that the young chap sitting there is her son. They've got the same hair, nose and eyes. And they both hold their teacups the same way. How old would you say he is? Twenty?"

"A son? But Miss Broadspoon never married."

"I'm only reporting what I see."

"He does look like her," agreed Pemberley. "Maybe he's her nephew?"

"The son of her identical twin, perhaps?"

"To my knowledge, she doesn't have a twin. I don't recall her having any siblings at all."

"A secret son, then?"

A movement beyond the window caught Churchill's attention. She peered out past the lace curtain to see a handful of people marching along the high street. They held placards and chanted something inaudible.

"Golly! Looks like someone's having a little protest. What a time to do it, just before Christmas. Wouldn't it be better to wait until the new year when everything's generally quieter and people have a little more time to listen to these things?"

"I wonder what they are protesting about?"

Churchill peered more closely at the placards. "I think one of the signs says, 'We want our jobs back'."

"I can see one that says, 'Pouch ruined our Christmas'," added Pemberley. "Oh dear. I think they may be the people Mr Pouch fired from his shop."

"How embarrassing. Look, people are stopping to watch them. It'll soon be common knowledge that he sacked everyone from his shop just before Christmas. It's not looking good for his reputation, is it? Even if he opens a new one, people will most likely shun it because they'll remember what he did to his previous employees."

"It's a difficult position to be in. That's why I would never want to run my own business."

"Me neither, Pembers. It's too much like hard work."

"But you do run your own business, Mrs Churchill, remember? Churchill's Detective Agency."

"Oh, so I do!" She chuckled. "How funny. Sometimes

we have so much fun that it doesn't feel like work at all. Don't you find that?"

"Occasionally."

Churchill turned her attention back to Miss Broadspoon and gave her a little wave.

"Oh, hello, Mrs Churchill, Miss Pemberley," she said. "How are you both?"

"We're very well, Miss Broadspoon," Churchill replied. "And you?"

"Well, I mustn't grumble, but I've got a bit of a twinge." She lifted a hand to the small of her back and winced.

"Oh dear."

"It kept me awake all night."

"Really?"

"I'm used to it now. I usually have some ailment or other keeping me up at night."

"I'm sorry to hear it."

"Did you hear about Mrs Higginbath being arrested? I didn't think she was capable of doing such a thing."

"She didn't do it."

"She didn't?"

"No. She was arrested, but there's no evidence that it was her."

"Oh! Inspector Mappin will have to start all over again, then."

"Exactly. Doesn't bode well, does it? I suppose the pool of suspects has been narrowed down now."

"Narrowed down to what?"

"The rest of us who were there that evening."

"Are you including us in that number, Mrs Churchill?"

"No, no. Present company excluded, of course." Churchill gave a cheery smile, knowing there was every possibility that Miss Broadspoon had poisoned Mrs Marrowpip.

"I suppose the only real suspect now is Dr Sillifant."

"Why's that?"

"Well, I only got to him by ruling out the others. You didn't do it, I didn't do it, Miss Pemberley didn't do it and Mrs Thonnings certainly wouldn't have murdered someone at her own Christmas dinner. Mr Pouch wouldn't have done it because he's Mrs Thonnings's man friend. Mrs Higginbath could have done it, but apparently she didn't, so all we have left is Dr Sillifant."

"I can't imagine him doing it either, Miss Broadspoon."

"Neither can I. Talking of Mr Pouch, there are some rather angry people standing outside, aren't there? I was speaking to some of them earlier, and they were telling me how awful it had been to lose their jobs just before Christmas. One man told me he has six children. He doesn't know how he's going to feed them on Christmas Day, apparently."

"Oh, no," said Churchill. "That really is most unfortunate. I hope Mr Pouch will give him a bit of money to buy something for Christmastime."

Miss Broadspoon wrinkled her nose. "I doubt it. Do you know what's made matters even worse?"

"No."

"He's taken over Enid's hardware store."

"Has he really?"

"Yes, only he hasn't taken his own staff with him because he's inherited Enid's employees. So Mr Pouch has acquired a bigger, better shop and his former employees are all out in the cold."

"Literally."

"Literally what?"

"It doesn't matter. Well, it's nice to see you, Miss

Broadspoon. We won't keep you and your companion any longer." Churchill gave the young man a pointed glance, indicating they hadn't been introduced yet.

"This is Crispin," said Miss Broadspoon.

Churchill noticed she didn't elaborate on the nature of their relationship.

Chapter 20

CHURCHILL AND PEMBERLEY stepped out of the tea rooms and watched the protest against Mr Pouch.

"You can't blame them for being angry, can you?" commented Churchill. "Let's go and take a peek inside the hardware shop. I can't say I ever went in while it was under Mrs Marrowpip's ownership."

"I was always in there," said Pemberley.

"Buying what?"

"Nails, screws, hammers... that sort of thing."

"For what?"

"Various activities. I also bought screwdrivers, sanding paper, hand drills..."

"Hand drills?"

"I prefer the double pinion ones... preferably with a keyless chuck."

"If only I knew what you were talking about, Pembers."

They reached the hardware store to find a variety of items laid out on trestle tables in front of the shop windows.

"A far better display than Mrs Marrowpip ever managed," commented Pemberley.

"Let's go inside," Churchill replied.

The well-stocked shop smelled of oil mixed with wood shavings. Grey-bearded Mr Pouch was humming to himself as he arranged a display of chisels.

"Good morning, Mr Pouch," said Churchill. "It's a surprise to see you here."

"Hello, Mrs Churchill. And Miss Pemberley. It is a bit of a surprise, isn't it? I had a discussion with Mrs Marrowpip's landlord and agreed to take over the lease. It would have been a shame to see her shop cease trading."

"It was very nice of you to step in."

"Thank you. I like to do my bit."

"We couldn't help but notice your disgruntled former employees protesting out on the high street."

"They're a nuisance, aren't they? Let's hope they get chilly and go home soon."

"Don't you any have space to employ them in your new enterprise here?"

"I'm afraid not. Oh, hello Mr Thurkell. Are you here for the drill bits you telephoned about?"

The two ladies took this as their signal to leave and went on their way. Churchill felt irritated that the conversation had been cut short.

"Miss Broadspoon seemed quite adamant that Dr Sillifant must have poisoned Mrs Marrowpip," commented Pemberley once they were back outside.

"Just a lack of imagination, I'd say. She only decided it was him because she'd eliminated everyone else in her mind."

"But surely you have to agree with her to some extent?"

"I don't have to agree with her at all."

"But if it wasn't Mrs Higginbath and it wasn't Dr Sillifant, who was it?"

"Miss Broadspoon herself, I shouldn't wonder."

"We'd need to find a reason to explain why she would do such a thing."

"Yes, that's something we'd need to look into."

"I wonder if Dr Sillifant's snowman is still standing."

"What's that got to do with anything?"

"I just find it rather interesting that everyone else's snowmen are being destroyed, yet his has remained standing."

"I imagine it's been destroyed by now but he's chosen not to make a fuss about it. Dr Sillifant isn't the sort of man to make a fuss."

"He may not want to make a fuss, but he could have helped our investigation by reporting it."

"That's a good point. We could plot all the snowmen attacks on a map, couldn't we? Especially after the two attacks last night. I reckon the snowman smasher is getting bolder."

"Maybe they smashed Dr Sillifant's, too?"

"I suppose there's only one way to find out. Let's go and have a look."

The two ladies and their dog strolled past the duck pond in the direction of Coldbone Hall. Churchill marvelled once again at its Tudor prettiness and wondered what it would be like to live in such a place... possibly with Dr Sillifant.

"His snowman's still standing," commented Pemberley. "Very interesting."

There was a fresh layer of snow on the snowman's top hat, suggesting it had been standing in place, without incident, for a few days.

"I should think there are plenty of people in the village who haven't had their snowmen smashed yet," replied Churchill.

"But our poor snowman was destroyed within hours of us building him. Was that just misfortune, would you say?"

"I imagine so. Or perhaps the snowman smasher didn't want to upset Dr Sillifant for some reason."

"But they'd happily upset plenty of other people, including children?"

"There is little logic to all this, Pemberley. Who knows what goes on in the warped mind of a snowman smasher? Perhaps Dr Sillifant's snowman will be targeted tonight. I think what you're implying, Pembers, is that Dr Sillifant could be the snowman smasher. Let me remove that thought from your mind once and for all. It's quite impossible that a man with such an esteemed reputation would stoop so low as to go about smashing up snowmen. He's much too refined and important for all that. He has far better things to concern himself with."

They heard the click of a door latch and the front door of Coldbone Hall opened. Dr Sillifant emerged in a dark-crimson velvet hat, smoking jacket and bow tie.

Churchill blushed a little. Then she remembered her dream about building the snowman with the doctor and blushed even more.

"Good morning, ladies!" he said with a grin. "I couldn't help but notice you standing out here in the cold. Would you like to come in for a cup of tea?"

"No, thank you," replied Pemberley. "We're busy."

"We'd be absolutely delighted to, Dr Sillifant," said Churchill, giving Pemberley a sharp look.

. . .

It was cosy in Dr Sillifant's front room, where a bright fire burned in the grate. The window overlooked the garden where the snowman stood.

"We were marvelling at how your snowman has remained standing all this time," commented Pemberley.

"Sir Dennis? Yes, he appears to have escaped the savaging so far."

"Our snowman was destroyed last night."

"Oh, really? That's dreadful news! You must have been extremely upset."

"We were, Dr Sillifant," replied Churchill. "We even tried to stay up to see if we could spot the attacker, but we fell asleep before they turned up."

"How awfully sad. Aren't some people terrible? Their fun will be over once the thaw comes, at least."

"We think it might have something to do with the Compton Poppleford Christmas Snowman Competition," said Churchill.

"As things stand, Dr Sillifant, yours might be the only entry," added Pemberley.

"Oh dear. Is it really that bad?"

"It certainly is," replied Churchill. "We've got to stop this person or the entire competition will be quite ruined."

"Let's hope not, eh?"

They paused while the housekeeper wheeled in a trolley with a pot of tea and a plate of mince pies on top.

"Can I tempt you to a mince pie, Mrs Churchill."

"I daresay you can, Doctor."

"Buttery pastry with plump, brandy-soaked fruits. And they're still warm from the oven."

Churchill's stomach gave an appreciative grumble. "It really doesn't get any better than that."

"It doesn't really, does it? I see you've brought your canine friend with you again. Would you like another bone, little chap?"

"No!" replied the two ladies in unison.

Dr Sillifant appeared quite taken aback. "Oh?"

"Thank you for your kind offer, Doctor," said Churchill, "but he really doesn't want another bone. He still hasn't finished the last one."

"Oh, I see. Well, how about I pour out the tea and you tell me how your investigation is going? I'm getting terribly bored, sitting about waiting for the Dorset Medical Council to tell me I can go back to work. Have you found out who the poisoner is yet?"

"Not yet. We initially thought Mrs Higginbath was the culprit."

"Oh, yes. On account of the angry words exchanged during Hunt the Thimble?"

"Yes, but mainly because Mrs Marrowpip had reported her for stealing."

"Gosh! It was Mrs Marrowpip who reported her, was it? Presumably, Mrs Higginbath wasn't too pleased about that and bumped her off!"

"That's what we thought, but it seems Mrs Higginbath is innocent. I suggested Inspector Mappin ask a poison expert to examine her bag for traces of the poison."

"A very good idea."

"But I don't think he's done that."

He shook his head. "Amateur."

"If Mrs Higginbath had been carrying poison in her handbag, do you think traces of it could be found?"

"Quite likely. It depends how the poison was packaged, of course. If it was wrapped in paper, traces could easily have been transferred to the lining of the handbag or the other contents therein. If the poison had been in a bottle, however, that would have kept it a little more contained. That said, the poisoner would have needed to open the packaging and handle the poison in some way. I didn't see anyone wearing gloves during our Christmas dinner, so I can only guess that the culprit took the risk of using their bare hands to administer it. In doing so, they would have transferred microscopic traces of poison onto their clothing. Let's imagine that Mrs Higginbath did keep the poison in her handbag. After administering the poison, she would have had to close her bag again, so I'm quite sure that traces of poison would have been left on the handle or clasp. Anywhere on the bag, in fact."

"You're so knowledgeable, Dr Sillifant," said Churchill. She bit into a mince pie, confident that she could listen to his dulcet tones all day long and never grow tired.

"I'm a trained doctor, Mrs Churchill."

"Have you any idea which poison it was that killed Mrs Marrowpip?"

"I had a little chat with the police doctor who attended. We were actually at medical school together. He suspected that the poison used was cyanide, also known as prussic acid."

"Golly!"

"It's a particularly unpleasant poison," he continued. "Once ingested, it displaces the oxygen in the bloodstream and travels around the body extremely quickly, causing the cells to die. Death is quick; sometimes instantaneous, I'm afraid."

"How do you retain all this knowledge, Doctor?"

"Years of experience." He adjusted his bow tie proudly. "You've probably ingested cyanide yourself, Mrs Churchill."

"Me? No, never."

"It's found in many plants, you see, including the pips

134

and stones of fruit. Surely you've accidentally swallowed an apple pip before now, Mrs Churchill?"

"I suppose I may have done."

"Apricot kernels?"

"What of them?"

"Don't go eating too many of those. As for almonds, eat the sweet ones at your leisure, but avoid the bitter ones."

"Do they have cyanide in as well?"

"Brimming over with the stuff! Planning a trip to the tropics any time soon?"

"No."

"You won't be consuming any cassava, then?"

"No."

"If you do venture there, enjoy it in moderation. In his poem, *Auguries of Innocence*, William Blake wrote that 'the strongest poison ever known came from Caesar's laurel crown.' He was suggesting that danger comes from those in power. However, like most literary geniuses, his words had a double meaning, as laurel contains high levels of cyanide."

"William Blake? I can't say I've met him yet. Does he live here in the village?"

Dr Sillifant chuckled. "That's a funny joke, Mrs Churchill."

She chuckled to herself, unsure what to make of his remark.

Pemberley clarified. "William Blake was a poet," she explained. "He was born in the eighteenth century."

"Oh, *that* William Blake," replied Churchill, immediately feeling foolish. She hoped the doctor wouldn't consider her ignorant. "I thought you were referring to another William Blake."

"It's not an uncommon name, is it? Now, back to Mrs

Higginbath. Not only could traces of poison have been transferred onto the handbag, but also onto her clothing. Perhaps even to where she was sitting at the table, and to her cutlery and crockery. Not enough to poison her, but certainly enough to be discoverable. If Inspector Mappin had had his wits about him when he attended the scene that evening, he would have called in a scientific expert to examine everyone's clothing and accessories. Handbags and what-have-you."

"Why didn't you suggest that to him, Dr Sillifant?" queried Pemberley.

"It's not for me to tell an officer of the law how to do his job, Miss Pemberley. All I can say is that the poisoner's lucky that Mappin wasn't very thorough."

"He's perfectly hapless, in fact," added Churchill. "Quite unlike you, Dr Sillifant."

"All this talk of Mrs Higginbath is rather misleading," said Pemberley, "I don't think she's the poisoner."

"Miss Broadspoon, then?" suggested Churchill.

"One of my favourite patients!" said the doctor. "Never!"

"One of your favourites, Dr Sillifant? Why so?"

"She's such a charming, erudite woman."

"Are we talking about the same person? Whenever I speak to her she can't help but moan about an ache or pain of some sort."

He chuckled. "That's Marigold for you. There's never a dull moment with her around."

Chapter 21

"I was thoroughly enjoying myself until Dr Sillifant mentioned Miss Broadspoon," said Churchill once the two ladies had left his house.

"I think it was you who brought her up, Mrs Churchill."

"Perhaps it was. But I wouldn't have done so if I'd known he would start singing her praises."

"What's wrong with that?"

"I just don't understand it. What did he call her? Charming and erudite. Pfft!"

"He must see a different side to her from the one we see."

"Clearly. Our visit had been fun up until that point. I do so enjoy listening to intelligent people. Don't you?"

"He is intelligent. But he also likes the sound of his own voice."

"If I had a voice like his, I would like it, too."

"You've got a bit of a thing for him, Mrs Churchill."

"A bit of a thing?"

"You carry a torch for him."

"I do not!"

"How can we fairly consider him a suspect if you're biased towards him?"

"I am *not* biased towards Dr Sillifant, Pembers."

"You seem rather keen to assume that he's neither the murderer nor the snowman smasher."

"I'm quite prepared to accept that he could be either."

"Or both, perhaps?"

"Both? Impossible! Besides, I very much doubt that he's responsible for either crime."

"He has an expert knowledge of poison," said Pemberley. "Very useful when you're planning to murder someone. And we've already agreed that he would find it easy to get hold of cyanide. All he has to do is ask the pharmacist, and it's handed over."

"I think you've got it in for him, Pembers. I can't deny that I enjoy Dr Sillifant's company, but I'm professional enough to know that we must consider him a suspect. I have a long list of reasons as to why I *wouldn't* consider him a suspect. A longer list than I might have for Miss Broadspoon, perhaps."

"I think we should go and speak to the Dorset Medical Council."

"About the complaint that was made against him?"

"Yes. In the same way that we spoke to Dorset's head librarian about the complaint made against Mrs Higginbath, we should ask the Dorset Medical Council who complained about Dr Sillifant."

"They'd never tell us."

"No, they may not. But in that case we'll have to find out by other means, just as we did at Dorset Central Library."

"Poking around in the head librarian's office is one

thing, Pembers, but doing something like that at the Dorset Medical Council is quite another."

"It's no different at all, Mrs Churchill! If we discover that Mrs Marrowpip complained about Dr Sillifant, he would have had a strong motive for poisoning her."

"But I think it's unlikely he's the culprit. I think such a visit would be a waste of our time."

"You told me you wouldn't be biased, Mrs Churchill, but I think you are being biased. If you're not going to visit the Dorset Medical Council to ask them, I will."

Churchill pondered this for a minute and realised she had been treating Dr Sillifant rather differently from the other Christmas party guests. "Fine," she conceded. "Let's go to Dorchester, yet again, and ask the Dorset Medical Council about the complaint. I'm sure it'll get us nowhere, but at least we'll have been as thorough as possible."

After another journey on the branch line, the two ladies reached Dorchester. The Dorset Medical Council occupied an austere, dark-stone building on a quiet, snowy side street.

"I think they purposefully design these places to look intimidating, don't they, Pembers? It makes one feel rather humbled about one's own level of education."

"I wouldn't worry about that," replied Pemberley. "I say we go in, ask the questions and see where that gets us."

"Indeed. Very forthright of you. Let's find out what they have to say for themselves."

The two detectives left Oswald at the door and stepped inside, their footsteps echoing on the marble floor of the cavernous entrance hall. Paintings of important-looking men in high collars hung on the walls and a faint medicinal smell lingered in the air.

"With whom may we speak regarding a complaint made against a Compton Poppleford doctor?" Churchill asked a dusty-looking man behind a high desk.

"You'd like to make a complaint?"

"No, we'd like to find out some details about an existing complaint."

"You can speak to the clerk, Mr Peebles."

The dusty-looking man gave the two ladies directions to his office, and they went off to find it.

"Well, this has been deceptively straightforward so far," said Churchill. "This next bit is where we're likely to run up against a brick wall, I reckon. And as I've already explained, Pembers, I'm not rummaging around in anyone's office again. How would we even distract the clerk here? There are no encyclopaedias to pull off shelves, that's for sure."

"Why not let me do the talking this time, Mrs Churchill? You always do the talking."

Churchill paused in the corridor. "But I thought you liked me doing the talking?"

"I normally do. But I've decided I'd like to step up to the challenge this time."

"Is that because you think my line of questioning may, for some inexplicable reason, be biased in favour of Dr Sillifant?"

"Yes, something like that."

"Are you sure, Pembers? This is the only chance we'll get to ask them. We don't want to blow it."

"What makes you think I'm going to blow it?"

"Just… rapport. It comes more naturally to some than to others."

"I can establish good rapport with people, Mrs Churchill. Just you wait and see."

"Very well. You do all the talking and I shall stand back and let you get on with it."

They knocked at a door labelled 'Mr Peebles'.

"Come in!" came the voice from within.

They stepped inside the office to find a young man with fair, curly hair and rosy cheeks sitting behind a desk piled high with papers.

"Oh, hello." He got to his feet. "How can I help you?"

Pemberley introduced them both. "You look very busy," she added.

"Yes, always very busy. Doctors don't stop for Christmas, you know. Do please take a seat."

"We'd like to ask you about a complaint you've received," said Pemberley. "We understand that Dr Sillifant of Compton Poppleford has been suspended from his duties while a complaint against him is being investigated."

"Yes, that rings a bell," replied Mr Peebles.

"Is it a serious complaint?"

"Not especially, as I recall it."

"Thank goodness," said Churchill.

"But it was decided that he should be suspended from his duties while the facts of the case were being established. You've just reminded me, actually. I think there's been a development in the case." He leafed through a pile of papers on his desk. "No, not in there." He leafed through another pile. "Or there." He got up and stepped over to a chair with another pile of papers on it. "Perhaps it's here."

"You could do with a proper filing system, Mr Peebles," commented Churchill.

"No need. I always know where everything is." He moved over to another stack of papers on top of a chest of drawers. "Perhaps it's here."

"This must be the ponderous, bureaucratic cog Dr

Sillifant was referring to," Churchill whispered to Pemberley.

"I'm sorry?" The clerk turned round.

"I was just remarking on the weather to Miss Pemberley."

The clerk returned to his desk. "Ah, here it is." He picked up a piece of paper from the top of a pile. "I remember now. I need to write to Dr Sillifant to inform him that the complaint has been dropped."

"Oh?" said Churchill. "Why's that?"

"It says here that the complainant is recently deceased."

Churchill and Pemberley exchanged a glance. "The complainant's name wasn't Mrs Marrowpip, by any chance?" asked Pemberley.

"As a matter of fact, it was."

Churchill felt an uncomfortable turn in her stomach.

"Mrs Enid Marrowpip made a complaint about Dr Sillifant a fortnight ago," continued Mr Peebles. "Apparently, he had been taking an undue interest in the value of her home."

Churchill snorted. "That sounds like a rather petty complaint to me."

"Yes, it's an odd one. We do get some funny complaints at times and we're obliged to look into all of them. There's no longer any need to deal with this one, given that Mrs Marrowpip has died. I shall get on with my letter to Dr Sillifant. If I catch today's post he'll receive it before Christmas. It's quite fortuitous that you ladies came down here to enquire about it!"

"He'll be extremely relieved to receive the letter," said Churchill. "And I'm so pleased we've been able to speed things along."

"Is there anything else I can help you with?" asked the clerk.

"Just one more thing," said Pemberley. "Was Dr Sillifant aware of who had made the complaint against him?"

"Yes, he was."

"When was he informed?"

"At the very outset, when we conducted our interview with him."

"I see."

"I have it on record here that he denied behaving in the manner the complainant had described. Anyhow, there's nothing more we can do about it. I'm sure he'll have a much more pleasant Christmas now."

"I'm sure he will," replied Pemberley.

The two ladies travelled back to Compton Poppleford on the train. The sun was setting on the snowy landscape rolling past the window, and Oswald snoozed on the seat opposite them.

"We should tell Inspector Mappin about our latest findings," said Pemberley.

Churchill felt uneasy that evidence seemed to be pointing to Dr Sillifant as the most likely murderer. She liked him too much to believe that he could be capable of such a thing. "Do you think so?"

"He needs to know that Mrs Marrowpip had made a complaint about Dr Sillifant, and that he therefore had a powerful motive for poisoning her. Not only did he have the motive, but he also had the means."

"Ah, but did he have the opportunity?"

"All of us at the dinner party that evening had the opportunity, Mrs Churchill. He fulfils all three criteria."

"We don't need to tell Inspector Mappin just yet, do

we? Remember what happened last time. He dashed off to make a hasty arrest and was found to be mistaken. You know who he'll take it out on if the same thing happens again. Us! There must be more evidence we can gather first. Or, better still, evidence against someone else."

"But don't you think it's rather suspicious that he took an undue interest in the value of Mrs Marrowpip's home? Especially when you consider that he already lives in a house left to him in a patient's will."

"Mrs Marrowpip probably took it the wrong way. It was likely to have been little more than a passing comment he made during a longer conversation. Had Mr Peebles and his friends at the Dorset Medical Council completed their investigation, they would have discovered there was nothing in it. What's becoming increasingly clear during the course of this investigation is that Mrs Marrowpip enjoyed telling tales on people."

"It's a shame the council was unable to complete the investigation. It's worked out rather conveniently for Dr Sillifant, hasn't it? I still think Inspector Mappin needs to know about this."

"If hapless Mappin was doing his job properly, he'd already know!" Churchill sighed. "I know we should probably mention it to him, but we need to make him promise not to go rushing out and locking people up in cells until he has more evidence. That would be very unfair, wouldn't it?"

"It wouldn't be unfair if he's the murderer. I would say that he thoroughly deserved it."

"Can we mention it to Inspector Mappin tomorrow?" Churchill glanced out at the darkening sky. "It's been a long day."

Chapter 22

Mrs Higginbath marched into Churchill and Pemberley's office the following morning.

"It's happened to me!" she announced. She wore a grey overcoat and a grey woollen hat was pulled over her grey hair.

"What's happened?" asked Churchill.

"My snowman. He's been smashed. I went to the trouble of building a snow wall around him. Six feet high, it was. I thought he'd be safe behind that, but it seems the snowman smasher's just ploughed their way through the wall and got to him."

Churchill was not accustomed to seeing Mrs Higginbath in an emotional state, but she thought she detected a tear in the former librarian's eye.

"Oh dear. I'm sorry to hear it."

"Are you going to come and take a look?"

Churchill was beginning to grow tired of the snowman smasher case. Despite their efforts, they didn't seem to have made any progress with it. "Now?"

"Yes, now. Come and see the damage they've caused."

"Very well."

"You don't seem particularly enthusiastic about it, Mrs Churchill. I read in the newspaper two days ago that people in the village are growing tired of your inability to solve this crime."

"The *Compton Poppleford Gazette* is a local rag and is unfit to be described as a newspaper, Mrs Higginbath. And besides, we're not unable to solve it, we're just a little busy at present. But at your insistence, we shall drop everything and come along to survey the destruction. Perhaps the snowman smasher has left a more useful clue this time."

A short while later, the two ladies and their dog found themselves standing with Mrs Higginbath in her garden.

"Judging by the vast heaps of snow on the ground, you clearly built an impressive wall," remarked Churchill. "I'm surprised they had any energy left to smash the snowman after battling their way through that."

"They must be filled with pure rage," added Pemberley.

"Golly!" said Churchill. "Do you think so?"

"Look at how the snowman's been trampled into the ground," her assistant replied.

Mrs Higginbath gave a sorrowful sniff as Churchill inspected the sadly familiar scene.

"We sometimes find that the smasher does something unpleasant with the head," said Churchill. "Have you found your snowman's head anywhere?"

Mrs Higginbath pointed at a nearby tree. High up in the boughs, a snowman's head with empty eye sockets stared down at them.

"Good grief!" said Churchill. "That really gives me the

shivers. Was there anything missing from your snowman? A scarf, perhaps?"

"A brooch."

"A brooch? That's an unusual item to put on a snowman."

"I realise that. I just wanted to do something a little different in the hope it would help me win the competition."

"Understandable. I'm sorry your brooch is missing."

"It was an inexpensive one that Mrs Thonnings gave me for Christmas last year. But I'm quite sad that it's lost."

"When we find the culprit, we'll make sure all the stolen hats, scarves, buttons, brooches and Easter bonnets are returned to their owners."

"Easter bonnets?"

"I'm afraid so." Churchill shook her head. "But right now, I really don't know how we're going to get to the bottom of this."

She looked down at the footprints, which were remarkably similar to the ones she and Pemberley had followed the previous day. "This trail will probably just lead back to the Wagon and Carrot."

"I noticed Dr Sillifant's snowman hadn't been knocked down when I was out walking near the duck pond yesterday," said Mrs Higginbath. "I know for a fact that his snowman's been there for a few days now."

"Yes, I suppose Coldbone Hall is just a bit out of the way. The snowman smasher clearly hasn't spotted Sir Dennis yet."

"Or maybe Dr Sillifant is the snowman smasher."

"I very much doubt it!" Churchill gave a dismissive laugh. "Dr Sillifant has far more important things to do than go about smashing up snowmen."

"He has a lot of time on his hands at the moment."

"Not for much longer. We've just discovered that he'll be returning to his work now that the complaint against him has been dropped."

"Why has it been dropped?"

"The complainant has died."

"Enid?"

"Now that you happen to mention it, yes, it was Mrs Marrowpip who made the complaint."

"Then why hasn't Dr Sillifant been arrested, like I was?"

"I really don't know, Mrs Higginbath. You'd have to ask Inspector Mappin about that."

"Inspector Mappin doesn't know," said Pemberley.

"He doesn't know that it was Enid who complained about Dr Sillifant?" said Mrs Higginbath. "Someone needs to tell him! I'll do it myself if you're not prepared to."

"It's all in hand," replied Churchill. "Miss Pemberley and I will be paying him a visit this morning, won't we, Miss Pemberley?"

"Will we?"

"Yes. Now then, Mrs Higginbath, I think you may be able to help us with another important line of enquiry. We observed something, or should I say *someone*, interesting in the tea rooms yesterday. Miss Broadspoon was sitting with a young man named Crispin."

"Oh, yes." Her lips pursed.

"Miss Broadspoon didn't happen to mention what her relationship to him was, but he bore a remarkable resemblance to her. Have you seen him about?"

Mrs Higginbath nodded.

"You seem to have been struck uncharacteristically dumb, Mrs Higginbath. Is there something you're not telling us?"

"Crispin is a regular visitor."

"And what is he in relation to her? A nephew?"

"Quite likely."

"Miss Pemberley doesn't recall Miss Broadspoon having any siblings."

"I couldn't possibly comment. I wouldn't know."

"But haven't you been friends with Miss Broadspoon for decades, Mrs Higginbath? Surely she must have discussed her family with you."

"It's none of my business," retorted Mrs Higginbath. "And it certainly isn't yours either, Mrs Churchill. Do you need anything more from the crime scene?"

"No, we've seen enough. Thank you, Mrs Higginbath."

"Crispin is Miss Broadspoon's son, isn't he?" Churchill said to Pemberley as they left Mrs Higginbath's home. "Mrs Higginbath was being rather cagey just then. I think she was trying to protect her friend."

"She might not have been."

"Oh, but she was. You know what she's like, Pembers. She's normally got far more to say on matters of that kind. Her reluctance to discuss it any further tells me everything I need to know."

"Even if Crispin is Miss Broadspoon's son," ventured Pemberley, "what does that have to do with anything?"

"Well, I suppose it doesn't, really. But I wonder how many people know the truth."

"I didn't know, so I think it may have been a well-kept secret all these years."

"Mrs Higginbath knows, though, doesn't she? The way she pressed her lips together just now confirms it. The question is, did Mrs Marrowpip know?"

"She may have done. She was good friends with Miss Broadspoon at one time."

"And then they fell out. That sort of knowledge can be a powerful tool, can't it, Pembers? It's the sort of knowledge that could be used against someone as a threat."

Chapter 23

As the two ladies and their dog turned into a lane near the high street, they caught sight of a familiar brown-whiskered police officer.

"Ah, there you are, Mrs Churchill and Miss Pemberley," said Inspector Mappin. I've been looking for you two."

"What is it now, Inspector?" Churchill asked. "We're not meddling, just in case you're about to accuse us of doing so."

"I wasn't going to tell you off, Mrs Churchill. In fact, I need your help."

"Well, that sounds rather intriguing. What can we help with?"

"My wife and I spent a pleasant few hours building our snowman for the Compton Poppleford Christmas Snowman Competition yesterday. However, we stepped outside this morning to find that it's been knocked to the ground."

Churchill groaned. "Not another one. We've just visited Mrs Higginbath's garden, where her snowman was felled. Let me guess… This heinous act was carried out during the hours of darkness, something unpleasant has happened to the head and an item that once adorned the snowman is now missing?"

"You're exactly right, Mrs Churchill. It seems you've established the snowman smasher's modus operandi."

Churchill felt quite impressed with this remark. "Modus operandi. I like that phrase, Inspector."

"Come and have a look at the crime scene."

The two ladies and their dog followed Inspector Mappin to his home, which was only a short distance away.

"Shall we tell Inspector Mappin about the complaint Mrs Marrowpip made against Dr Sillifant?" Pemberley whispered.

"A little later, Pembers. Let's deal with the matter at hand first."

"Dr Sillifant might receive his letter today. He needs to be arrested before he can start working again."

"If he's guilty, that is! And the chances are, he isn't. Anyway, let's concentrate on Mappin's snowman for now and we can discuss that topic with him a little later."

The inspector led them to the rear of his pretty timbered house.

He pointed to a bird table. "The head's been left over there. Can you see it? Just staring back at us."

"Creepy," remarked Churchill. She surveyed the familiar heap of snow and footprints. "What was taken from your snowman?"

"Something of significant sentimental value, actually. My old helmet from my days as a constable."

"Oh, how very unfortunate. I imagine that was something you treasured."

"It was, in fact. I do hope that you'll be able to retrieve it for me, Mrs Churchill."

"Why did you build a snowman for the Compton Poppleford Christmas Snowman Competition if you're the judge, Inspector?"

"I thought it would be a bit of fun. I'll obviously make sure that I don't win it."

"You can't, anyway, seeing as your snowman's been flattened."

"That's true." He glanced sadly at the mound of snow. "There are going to be very few entries indeed at this rate."

"That's just what the snowman smasher wants," commented Pemberley.

"They've been doing this for a while now, haven't they?" said Inspector Mappin. "You'd have thought that at least one or two useful clues would have been left by now."

"Other than the footprints, Inspector, we have nothing substantial to go on."

The police officer placed his foot next to one of the footprints. "I would say that I have average-sized feet for a man," he said, "and these footprints are much the same size as mine. I would say that the assailant is neither particularly short nor particularly tall. Distinctly average."

"That doesn't really narrow things down for us, does it?" Churchill said.

"I took it upon myself to follow the footprints to see if I could work out where they came from," he added. "But they just led to the high street, where they got mixed up with all the other footprints. It was impossible to follow them from there."

"That's exactly the same trouble we've had in trying to identify the suspect."

"Well, these atrocities won't go on for much longer. I'll

be judging the Compton Poppleford Christmas Snowman Competition tomorrow."

"In which case, lots of people will probably attempt to build new snowmen today," said Pemberley.

"Which can only mean one thing," replied Churchill. "The snowman smasher will be out tonight, destroying as many snowmen as possible! I think we need to go out on patrol."

"What an excellent idea," said Inspector Mappin. "If we all keep a lookout, we'll almost certainly catch them."

"Good idea, Inspector. How jolly nice it is that we're finally in agreement about something. We shall leave you to it now and be on our way."

"There is something else, though," said Pemberley. "We've picked up a little nugget of information that might be useful as part of your investigation into the death of Mrs Marrowpip."

The inspector frowned. "You're not still meddling in that case, are you?"

"Please hear us out, Inspector. Mrs Churchill and I were in Dorchester yesterday and we just happened to be passing the Dorset Medical Council offices."

The inspector folded his arms. "Just passing, eh?"

"Yes. Aware that Dr Sillifant had been suspended by the Dorset Medical Council, we made the briefest of enquiries within. They were very helpful indeed and told us that the patient who had made the complaint against Dr Sillifant was none other than Enid Marrowpip. And what's more, Dr Sillifant knew she was the one who had complained about him."

Inspector Mappin raised an eyebrow, then shook his head. "No, I don't want to consider this piece of information. Thank you all the same."

"Why not?" asked Pemberley. "It gives Dr Sillifant a

strong motive for murdering Mrs Marrowpip."

"The last time I followed a lead like this, poor Mrs Higginbath had to spend a night in the police cells. Chief Inspector Llewellyn-Dalrymple took a rather dim view of it all, I must say. I shall make a note of what you've told me, but I've no intention of acting on it immediately. More evidence is needed."

"It absolutely is, Inspector," said Churchill. "I don't, for one minute, believe that Dr Sillifant would have harmed Mrs Marrowpip. We thought we'd better mention it all the same, seeing as we'd come across this interesting piece of information purely by chance."

Churchill and Pemberley made their way along the high street.

"Isn't Inspector Mappin even going to speak to Dr Silli- fant about it?" asked Pemberley. "I think he's missing an important opportunity if not."

"He's already spoken to everyone who was at the party, hasn't he? It's not as if he's completely ruled him out as a suspect."

"Unlike you, Mrs Churchill."

"I haven't completely ruled him out either, but I think he's probably the least likely of the remaining suspects."

"Who would you say is the most likely?"

"I'm not sure." Churchill's eye caught sight of the hardware store. "Although it appears that Mrs Marrow- pip's death has proved rather convenient for Mr Pouch, wouldn't you say, Pembers?"

"Do you think he poisoned her so he could have her shop?"

"It's an interesting possibility, isn't it? I think we need to go and speak to our good friend Mrs Thonnings."

Chapter 24

Mrs Thonnings greeted Churchill and Pemberley cheerily as they stepped inside her haberdashery shop. "I expect you've come to see my new stock of Christmas ribbons! They're just over here."

Before they could argue with her, Mrs Thonnings showed them the display. The colourful ribbons were printed with an array of festive patterns.

"I would like the one with Christmas trees on it," said Pemberley. "Just enough to tie a little bow around Oswald's collar."

"What a lovely idea, Miss Pemberley." Mrs Thonnings cut a length of ribbon for her.

"One of these has plum puddings printed on it," commented Churchill.

"Isn't it delightful? You could use it to wrap a gift or trim a Christmas garment."

"Plum pudding reminds me of the sad event that took place at your Christmas dinner, Mrs Thonnings."

"Oh dear." The haberdasher's face fell. "Now you put it like that, I suppose it's not so delightful." She picked up the spool of ribbon, walked over to the counter and tossed it into the bin.

"I don't think there's any call to be that drastic," said Churchill. "Plenty of customers who weren't at your Christmas dinner would be happy to buy it, I'm sure."

"But I shall be reminded every time I look at it."

"I see. Well, hopefully the investigation will be resolved soon. Perhaps you could keep it back for next year?"

"No, I couldn't possibly. It's tainted now." Mrs Thonnings peered into the bin. "A wet teabag has already soaked into it."

"Shame," said Churchill, wishing she had never mentioned it. "Anyway, it rather surprised us to discover that Mr Pouch is running Mrs Marrowpip's hardware store."

"Yes. That's turned out to be a bit of luck, hasn't it? He had a word with the landlord, who didn't want the shop to be sitting empty, particularly at a busy time like Christmas. So Bernard's taken it on."

"Which means that Mr Pouch has benefited from Mrs Marrowpip's death," said Pemberley.

"Oh, no, he hasn't benefited at all. He's dreadfully upset about it. We both are. But it was the best he could do in a difficult situation. I'm sure you agree, ladies, that it would have been terribly sad for her shop to be sitting there, closed up. And Mr Pouch had just closed his own shop, so the poor residents of Compton Poppleford would have had to travel all the way over to South Bungerly for their hardware supplies. It really has worked out very well for everyone."

"Except for Mrs Marrowpip," said Churchill.

"Of course. It didn't work out well for her, and that's most regrettable. But there's not a lot we can do about that now, is there? All we can do is find the person who poisoned her and bring them to justice."

"The person who poisoned Mrs Marrowpip did it for a reason. The most likely reason is that she was an inconvenience in some way. The poisoner clearly decided it would help his or her cause if she were removed."

"Now you put it like that, I suppose she was rather an inconvenience to some people."

"But the question is, who?" said Churchill.

"Well, I know it's wrong to point a finger at a friend, but Enid *was* in the way of Mrs Higginbath and her librarian job."

"She also made a complaint about Dr Sillifant, which resulted in him being suspended from his job," added Pemberley.

"Really?" exclaimed Mrs Thonnings.

"Yes, but we don't think that's quite so relevant, do we, Miss Pemberley?"

"But that's two people who had a motive." Mrs Thonnings considered this for a moment. "Dr Sillifant? I never would have thought it."

"Me neither," replied Churchill. "I really don't think it was him."

"I do," said Pemberley.

"What do you know about young Crispin, the chap who's here visiting Miss Broadspoon at the moment?" Churchill asked the haberdasher.

"He visits her every Christmas, I believe he's a family member."

"Yes, we gleaned that. He bears an uncanny resemblance to her, doesn't he?"

"Now you come to mention it, I suppose he does. It must be the way the Broadspoons look."

"Do you happen to know exactly who he is in relation to her?" Churchill probed.

"I don't, I'm afraid."

"We put it to Mrs Higginbath that Crispin could be Miss Broadspoon's son. What do you make of that?"

Mrs Thonnings fell quiet for a moment. "She never married, so it's quite impossible."

"But you know from your own experience, Mrs Thonnings, that it wouldn't be impossible, don't you? Crispin could be her son."

"Goodness! I can't imagine Marigold ever being as wayward as that. Could he really be her son?"

"We don't know who else he could be," replied Churchill, "and she remained tight-lipped on the nature of her relationship with him."

"He does have the same nose, doesn't he? And come to think of it, they both wear those thick-lensed glasses. And the hair is wavy on both counts, too. Well I never!"

"I don't suppose you know who Mr Marrowpip might have had an affair with, do you?"

"What's that got to do with anything?"

"I'm just trying to fill the gaps in my knowledge," Churchill replied.

"I'm afraid I don't know who it was. The fellow just left, and then we all found out later he'd gone off with another woman. I believe he went to Dorchester. Enid didn't like to talk about it."

"Could it have been Miss Broadspoon?"

"No, I don't think so."

"Perhaps Crispin is the son of Miss Broadspoon and Mr Marrowpip."

Mrs Thonnings gasped. "I consider it unlikely, but I suppose anything could be the case, couldn't it? I don't know how old Crispin is. He looks to be about twenty."

"How long ago did Mr Marrowpip leave his wife?" asked Churchill.

"I'd say it was about five years ago."

"The timing doesn't fit, then. But perhaps he had an affair with Miss Broadspoon twenty or so years ago?"

"She certainly had an affair with someone twenty years ago if Crispin is her son. But why Mr Marrowpip?"

"I'm trying to work out whether there was any animosity between Miss Broadspoon and Mrs Marrowpip," Churchill explained.

"There certainly was a bit of animosity between them. I can't say that I ever discovered the full reason, but perhaps that would explain it. You think Marigold could have poisoned Enid, do you? I would have thought it more likely to have been the other way around if it was going to happen at all. It would have made more sense for Enid to poison Marigold as an act of revenge for the affair with her husband. But for something that happened twenty years ago, if at all? I can't imagine that having anything to do with Enid's death."

"Mrs Marrowpip enjoyed complaining about people," said Pemberley. "She seemed to like dropping everyone in it, didn't she? We've seen it with Mrs Higginbath and with Dr Sillifant. Perhaps she told someone that Miss Broadspoon had given birth to a son out of wedlock."

"Yes, Pembers!" said Churchill. "That may well have been what happened! Or maybe she had threatened to tell someone? That certainly would have given Miss Broadspoon a reason to silence her, wouldn't it?"

"Golly!" said Mrs Thonnings. "That means three of the guests at my Christmas dinner must have been annoyed with Mrs Marrowpip. Or at least *might* have been annoyed. With hindsight, I suppose it was the wrong combination of people to invite, wasn't it? I wasn't aware that all this was going on."

"She was also rather rude to Mr Pouch, wasn't she, Mrs Thonnings?"

"Yes, she was. And to think I only invited her because I felt sorry for her. I wish I hadn't now, and then she wouldn't have been poisoned at my Christmas dinner, and I wouldn't have become the focal point for all this dreadful attention over the past few days. I had a photographer from the *Compton Poppleford Gazette* poking his camera lens in through my shop window yesterday. Then he had the cheek to come inside! I had to shoo him out."

"Mrs Marrowpip was rude to Mr Pouch, but he appears to have done quite well for himself since she passed away," said Churchill. "He now has a nice new hardware store on a busy shopping street. Something he didn't have before."

"Yes. Every cloud has a silver lining, I suppose."

"Do you think he'd always had his eye on that hardware store, Mrs Thonnings?"

"No, I think he was quite happy with the shop he had. Until he realised it wasn't making much money."

"And after that he realised he would make far more if he owned Mrs Marrowpip's store?"

"Well, I suppose... Just a minute, Mrs Churchill." Mrs Thonnings's eyes narrowed. "You're not suggesting what I think you're suggesting, are you? Bernard would never have poisoned Mrs Marrowpip. What an awful thought! If you're going to consider that as a possibility, you can get out of my shop this very moment!"

"We have to consider everyone at your Christmas dinner a suspect, Mrs Thonnings."

"Do you indeed? Then you might as well consider me, too. Perhaps I had a motive for poisoning Enid? And what about you, Mrs Churchill, and you, Miss Pemberley? The pair of you could have done it, for all I know. I don't want to discuss this any more. Get out of my shop!"

"Well, I think it's safe to say that we've upset Mrs Thonnings," said Churchill as they walked along the high street.

"She didn't like our suggestion that Mr Pouch might have poisoned Mrs Marrowpip."

"No, she didn't. But you have to admit, Pembers, that he has a strong motive. It's a shame Mrs Thonnings can't see it."

"Love is blind."

"It certainly is. Now, do you happen to know where Miss Broadspoon lives?"

"I think she's in Delphinium Cottage."

"You said that as if I'm supposed to know where it is."

"It's on Jasmine Lane."

"Where's that?"

"Just over on the other side of the park, Mrs Churchill. Follow me."

Chapter 25

As THE TWO ladies made their way to Delphinium Cottage, Churchill noticed people in their gardens, balling up mounds of snow and constructing snowmen.

"There's a frenzy of snowman-building afoot," she said. "The snowman smasher's going to have a lot of fun tonight, aren't they? What a horrible person they must be. The more I think about them, the more dreadful and despicable I consider their actions to be. Look at all these people having fun." She waved at a small girl rebuilding a snowman with her father. "And to think that the smasher will be out destroying them all tonight. It makes me incandescent with rage when I think about it. It makes my blood boil."

"It's mean-spirited," agreed Pemberley. "Especially at Christmastime."

Delphinium Cottage was a small, terraced house with a wonky chimney stack. The two ladies walked up the garden path and knocked at the door.

It was Crispin who answered. He gave them a weak smile.

"Good afternoon, young man," said Churchill. "We'd like to speak to Miss Broadspoon."

He invited them in, and the two ladies found themselves inside a small, low-ceilinged sitting room where Miss Broadspoon lay on the settee. A limp Christmas tree adorned with a handful of baubles stood in the window.

"Oh, hello Mrs Churchill and Miss Pemberley. And I see you've got your little dog with you." She sat herself up and patted Oswald on the head. "I do like his Christmas bow tie. I must apologise for my slovenly appearance. I've got another one of my heads."

"I'm sorry to hear it, Miss Broadspoon," said Churchill. "We'll be as quick as possible, so as not to disturb you too much."

"Oh, it's all right. I'm so used to the pain that I can usually soldier on regardless."

"That's the spirit! I take it you're not well enough to be outside building a snowman for the Compton Poppleford Christmas Snowman Competition tomorrow?"

"I hate snow," she responded. "It's far too cold and wet for my liking."

"Oh, I see."

"And I hate snowmen even more. There's something rather strange and freakish about snow being shaped into a human form, don't you think? They startle me whenever I go about my business around the village. Sometimes I think it's a person staring at me. Then I discover it's even worse; it's a snowman with an icy white face and dark, satanic eyes."

"Cripes. They're only supposed to be a bit of fun," replied Churchill. "And besides, the snowfall never lasts long, does it? Soon it will all be melted. I think it's a good idea to enjoy it while it's here."

"You'll never convince me," replied Miss Broadspoon.

"I hope I haven't disappointed you if that was your reason for visiting."

"No, absolutely, not." Churchill was conscious that Crispin was in the room and realised she would have to choose her words carefully. It was possible that the young man himself was unaware that he was Miss Broadspoon's son. "We were just wondering how well you knew Mr Marrowpip," she said.

"Mr Marrowpip? I haven't seen him for about five years. Not since he ran off with Mrs Maggie Grainger."

"Was there a divorce, do you know?"

"Yes, there was."

"What about before he ran off with Mrs Grainger? Did you know him well then?" Churchill watched Miss Broadspoon's expression closely, looking for any hint that she might be trying to hide a fondness for him.

"I used to have tea with Enid every Tuesday afternoon, so I sometimes saw him when he returned from work. But I didn't know him very well."

"And that was the only time you saw him? When you went to have tea with Mrs Marrowpip?"

"Yes, that was the only time. Why do you ask?"

"We're just trying to find out a little more about him. He went off with a Mrs Grainger, you say?"

"Yes, the school headmistress."

"Heavens! That must have been a bit of a scandal."

"It wasn't, really. Very few people knew about it."

"I didn't know about it," replied Pemberley. "I assumed she left the village because she'd been caught beating her pupils."

"She doesn't sound very nice at all," remarked Churchill.

"It was in the *Compton Poppleford Gazette* and everything," said Miss Broadspoon. "She left in disgrace. But she also left to be with Mr Marrowpip, though not many people realised that. I think it's just as well that she moved to Dorchester. At least all the children in Compton Popple-ford are safe now."

"Do you happen to know what became of Mr Marrowpip?"

"I couldn't tell you."

"Are you absolutely sure about that, Miss Broadspoon? You weren't on friendly terms with him at all?"

"No. Why would you think I was?"

"If it's true that Mr Marrowpip had a fling with Mrs Grainger, it's possible he may have had flings with other women in the village, too."

"Well, if he did, I certainly didn't know about it."

"Thank you for all your help, Miss Broadspoon." Churchill smiled at Crispin. "How long will your guest be staying with you?"

"Crispin will be staying here for three weeks, as he does every Christmas."

"How nice. Will any other family be joining you?"

"No, it'll just be me and Crispin."

"I see." Churchill turned to the young man. "What about your family, Crispin? Will they be missing you over Christmas?"

He stared at Churchill for a moment, then at Miss Broadspoon. His eyes widened, as if he wasn't sure what to say.

"Oh, my head!" exclaimed Miss Broadspoon, clasping her forehead. "It suddenly feels a lot worse!"

Churchill persevered. "Mrs Marrowpip was a good friend of yours, wasn't she, Miss Broadspoon?"

"Yes, she was."

"But the two of you fell out over something, didn't

you?" This was a guess, but Churchill felt sure it was a good one.

"We had our disagreements from time to time." Miss Broadspoon rubbed at her head and exhaled loudly.

"But how about recently? How about shortly before she died?"

"I don't like talking about that, because it's upsetting."

"I realise that, Miss Broadspoon. It's always upsetting when someone is murdered. But for the sake of our investigation, it would help if you could tell us just how friendly you and Mrs Marrowpip were at the time of her death."

"I don't see how that has anything to do with your investigation. And besides, why is it *your* investigation? I thought Inspector Mappin was investigating Enid's death."

"He is, but sometimes he needs a bit of help. Now, seeing as you haven't answered my question, Miss Broadspoon, I can only assume that the two of you were having words about something at the time of Mrs Marrowpip's death."

"As a matter of fact we were, but it was nothing important."

"Are you sure about that?"

"Mrs Marrowpip was once a good friend, but the trouble with her was she liked to tell tales."

"Yes, we've discovered that. She had Mrs Higginbath and Dr Sillifant suspended from their jobs."

"Did she really? There you go, you see. I'm afraid she had a bit of a nasty streak."

"Did she ever threaten to tell tales on you, Miss Broadspoon?"

"Why do you ask that?"

"Because she seems to have done it to everyone else."

Miss Broadspoon's lower lip wobbled a little. "There

was something she threatened to tell people about, but I don't want to go into it. It's too personal."

"Absolutely, Miss Broadspoon. We understand. Something related to your family, perhaps?"

"I really wouldn't like to say."

"Right. I shouldn't like to bother you any further while you've got one of your heads, but thank you for speaking so frankly."

The two ladies went on their way.

"I'd say that Miss Broadspoon seems suspicious on all counts, Pembers."

"Really? Are you sure you're not just a little biased against her because Dr Sillifant described her as charming and erudite?"

"I wish you would stop getting all these ideas in your noggin about me being biased. I think Miss Broadspoon may be the poisoner because Mrs Marrowpip was threatening to tell tales of a personal nature on her. That could only be something to do with Crispin being her son, don't you think? Also, have you noticed how much she hates snow and snowmen? I've never met anyone with such a strong dislike for snow before. I have a strong suspicion that she's our snowman smasher."

"I can see why she might be in the frame for both crimes," replied Pemberley, "but is she really a poisoner?"

"We need evidence, don't we? With regard to the poisoning, I'll have a think about that. But with regard to the snowman smashing, I think we need to carry out some surveillance. Tonight will be the night when the snowman smasher does his or her best to ruin all the rebuilt entries. If Miss Broadspoon is the culprit, we should be able to catch her red-handed."

Chapter 26

ONCE NIGHT HAD FALLEN, Churchill and Pemberley met at the end of Jasmine Lane. A solitary lamppost illuminated the large snowflakes slowly floating down from the dark sky.

"You look well wrapped up, Pembers," commented Churchill.

Only her assistant's eyes were visible, with her hat pulled down low and her scarf wrapped around the lower portion of her face. "We have to be." Pemberley's voice was muffled by layers of wool. "We could be out all night."

"Let's hope not, but you never know. I've also wrapped up well, for that very reason. Between you and me, I'm wearing a pair of Detective Chief Inspector Churchill's long johns beneath my Harris Tweed skirt. I've tucked them into my wellington boots, but I'm sure no one will notice them in the dark."

"You can never wrap up too warmly."

"Absolutely not, especially on a night like this. Now then, Pembers. Let's take up position near Delphinium Cottage and keep a close eye on Miss Broadspoon."

The two ladies and Oswald found a handy spot beneath a tree, its snow-laden branches casting enough shadow to shield them from the lamplight.

"Looks like she's at home," Churchill whispered. "The lights are on."

"Unless she's already out smashing up snowmen and that's just Crispin at home."

"Good point."

"If she does turn out to be the snowman smasher, how do we explain the footprints? They appear to have come from a man-sized boot."

"Perhaps she borrows Crispin's boots?" Churchill mused.

"And wears them to the Wagon and Carrot?"

"That's an interesting thought. We'll need to ask in there to establish whether Miss Broadspoon has ever been seen wearing oversized boots at the bar."

"Perhaps Crispin is the snowman smasher?" suggested Pemberley.

"He could be. But we don't know whether he has the same hatred for snow and snowmen as his mother."

"It's probably been passed down through the family."

"It may well have been. These things often are."

"I'm cold," said Pemberley.

"If everything goes to plan, we won't be waiting here much longer. If Miss Broadspoon's plan is to smash all the newly built snowmen, she'll need to get started soon. There are a lot of targets to attack."

"Do you think she's determined to destroy all of them?"

"It certainly looks that way. Few have remained standing for more than a day up to now."

"Apart from Dr Sillifant's."

"There's no denying that his snowman is a bit of an anomaly."

"Maybe Miss Broadspoon has a soft spot for Dr Sillifant."

"I wouldn't be surprised," Churchill replied.

"Perhaps Crispin is Dr Sillifant's son."

"No! That's completely impossible, Pembers. Dr Sillifant could never have been interested in Miss Broadspoon in that way."

"Why not? We already know he's rather fond of her. And she's a hypochondriac, so she's probably always attending his practice."

"I'm sure she is, but that doesn't mean the two are conducting an affair, or have ever done so in the past. She's not his type."

"How do you know that?"

"He's the *intellectual* sort, that's why."

"That doesn't rule her out, though."

"I realise that. But if I explain further, Pembers, you'll probably accuse me of being a snob or something along those lines."

Oswald trotted away from them and headed up Miss Broadspoon's garden path.

"Fetch your dog back, please, Pemberley. We can't have him giving us away."

"Oswald!" Pemberley called.

"Don't shout, Pembers!"

"How else am I supposed to get him back?"

"Go and fetch him!"

Oswald now stood in front of Miss Broadspoon's door, sniffing at the snowy step. "I don't want to fetch him," said Pemberley. "I might be seen."

"Then perhaps you should have put him on a lead so this couldn't have happened in the first place."

Pemberley sighed, then walked cautiously up Miss Broadspoon's path, checking to her left and right that no one was watching.

She was just bending down to pick up the little dog when the front door opened.

Churchill gasped.

Miss Broadspoon stood in the doorway, wrapped up in a thick coat with a hat and scarf. "Miss Pemberley?"

Churchill prayed her assistant would be able to talk her way out of the situation.

"I was just walking past your cottage when my dog ran up your path," said Pemberley. "He must have remembered coming here earlier."

"I suppose he must."

"I'll be on my way now. Sorry for bothering you, Miss Broadspoon."

Pemberley walked back over to Churchill with Oswald in her arms.

"Walk on past!" hissed Churchill, waving her away.

"Why?"

"You're supposed to be walking past Miss Broadspoon's cottage. Don't give me away, too!"

"Oh, yes."

However, Miss Broadspoon had already followed Pemberley down the path. "Hello, Mrs Churchill. What are you doing here?"

Churchill gritted her teeth and stepped out onto the path. "I was just waiting for Miss Pemberley to fetch her dog. How are you this fine evening, Miss Broadspoon?"

"I've been better. I thought I'd come out for a bit of air. The evenings are so much nicer in the summer when it's warm and the sun's still shining, aren't they?"

"They are, but I also like this time of year. After a

chilly constitutional, one can happily retire to the fireside with a mug of hot cocoa."

"The last time I had a cup of cocoa I scalded my tongue."

"I'm very sorry to hear it, Miss Broadspoon. Come along, now, Miss Pemberley. We'd better be on our way."

The two ladies hurried to the end of the lane, with Pemberley carrying Oswald in her arms.

"Darn it!" muttered Churchill. "Now we can't follow Miss Broadspoon to find out what she's up to. She's seen us!"

"We could still follow her."

"Not very easily. She's already seen us hanging about outside her house, so she'll know that we're on to her. If she *is* the snowman smasher, she's going to be extra cautious now. If only you hadn't let your dog run up her garden path, Pembers. Did you happen to look at the boots she was wearing?"

"No, I forgot. Did you?"

"I forgot, too."

"What do we do now?"

"Let's have a little wander about. Hopefully we can still catch Miss Broadspoon in the act."

They turned into Primrose Lane.

"Who goes there?" came a stentorian voice.

They started. It was then that they caught sight of a pale face peering down at them from above a snow-covered hedge.

"Good grief! Who's that?"

"Is that you, Mrs Churchill?"

"Yes."

"It's only me, Mrs Craythorne. I'm keeping guard."

"Goodness! All night?"

"I have no choice." She stepped out from behind the hedge to reveal the broom handle in her hand. "And if I catch sight of the snowman smasher, I'll smash him in with this."

"Golly. *He* might be a *she*, you know."

"Then I'll smash *her* in with this."

"There's probably no need for violence, Mrs Craythorne. The fact that you're present will probably be deterrent enough for the snowman smasher. Whoever it is clearly doesn't want to be identified."

"I hope you're right. I take no pleasure in violence, but I'm rather desperate to win the Compton Poppleford Christmas Snowman Competition. And if I'm to stand a chance, I have to be prepared to defend my snowman."

"Absolutely, Mrs Craythorne. Good luck. Miss Pemberley and I are also on patrol this evening, so if you see anyone acting suspiciously, just holler and we'll come running."

"Thank you, Mrs Churchill." Mrs Craythorne held out her hand and Churchill shook it. "Together, we'll catch that wretched smasher!"

As Churchill and Pemberley continued on their way, they encountered the family Churchill had seen rebuilding their snowman the previous day.

"I've got a powerful torch," the mother told them. "Watch this!"

Churchill was momentarily blinded by the flashlight shining in her face.

"No one likes that, do they?" the woman asked.

"No, they don't."

"We're also keeping an eye on Mrs Harris's snowman next door. She's gone back inside to warm up for a bit."

"I'm not surprised. Rather chilly, isn't it? It's very kind

of you to look out for Mrs Harris's snowman. With a bit of luck, we'll catch the snowman smasher in the next hour or so. Then everybody can get back inside and warm up."

The two ladies walked on. "I must say that I admire the community spirit the snowman smasher seems to have brought out in everyone. Don't you, Pembers? There's nothing like a common adversary to bring everyone together, is there? Practically every snowman is guarded, it seems. What a wonderful community response."

They passed Mr Groggins as they walked along Pemberley's street.

"That snowman smasher will have to take me down before he takes my snowman down," he said proudly.

"That's the spirit, Mr Groggins," Churchill replied.

A few minutes later they passed Mr Pouch's garden and noticed him sitting on a deckchair next to his snowman. "Evening, ladies!" he called out. "What have you done to upset Gladys?"

Churchill thought it best to plead ignorance. "We've upset her, have we?"

"Yes, but she won't tell me what happened. Never mind. She'll come out with it soon enough."

"We're on patrol, looking out for the snowman smasher, Mr Pouch. Give us a shout if you see him. Or her!"

"I will do!"

A familiar figure approached as they headed in the direction of the church.

"It's her!" whispered Churchill. "Miss Broadspoon! Observe the way she's glancing into every garden, Pembers. She's looking for a snowman to smash!" She couldn't resist a chuckle. "I imagine she's struggling this evening, given that everyone is out guarding their snowmen."

As they drew nearer, Churchill greeted her. "Enjoying your walk, Miss Broadspoon?"

"Not really. It's very cold. Although the air does seem to have cleared my head a little."

"Are you heading home shortly, or will you be continuing your walk for a little while longer?"

"I shall go on a little longer, I think. I don't feel tired enough to go back just yet."

"You have impressive stamina, Miss Broadspoon. I can see you promenading about the village all night at this rate!"

"I have done that before, on occasion. I'm not a great sleeper, you see. Sometimes it's better to spend the night roaming the streets than being tucked up in bed, wide awake."

Churchill was about to respond when a distant shout rang out. "What was that, Miss Pemberley? Someone must have seen the smasher! Which direction did it come from?"

"Near the duck pond, by the sound of it!"

They bid farewell to Miss Broadspoon and dashed off as quickly as they could through the snow.

"Do you think someone's seen them?" puffed Churchill, lagging behind Pemberley.

"They must have done. I can't think why else they would have shouted out like that."

Churchill's legs were already aching. "This snow's rather tricky to run in, isn't it? It's difficult not to find oneself slippy-sliding all over the place."

They rounded a corner and continued along Mucklebun Lane.

"Catch them!" came a shout. A dark figure dashed across the top of the lane ahead of them.

"Was that the smasher, Pembers?"

"It was certainly someone."

The two ladies and their dog ran to the top of the lane and turned left, heading in the direction in which the dark figure had run.

"Follow those footprints!" commanded Churchill.

Although the fleeing suspect's trail mingled with several others along the lane, Churchill was sure she was able to identify the boot prints they had seen so many times before.

Up ahead, the figure turned right.

"I can't keep up with them," puffed Churchill. "Can you, Pembers?"

"I'll try, but it's hard work in this snow."

"Can't you set Oswald on them?"

"He's not trained to hunt," replied Pemberley. "He's a Spanish water dog with a touch of terrier and a splash of spaniel, remember?"

"Well, he could do with being some sort of hound right now," huffed Churchill, struggling for breath. "It's not fair… to expect two ladies in the… the autumn of their years… to chase down a… snowman smasher."

They reached the turning the snowman smasher had run down and followed the footprints along a little lane. To their dismay, it led out onto the high street. The footprint trail was lost.

Churchill's bosom heaved with exhaustion. "They must be in…"

"The Wagon and Carrot?"

"Yes! You… you read my mind." Churchill tried to catch her breath as she and Pemberley trudged towards the pub. "I'll need a brandy when we get in there."

They pushed open the door to the pub and were surprised to find it unusually quiet inside.

"It's normally filled to the rafters in here," observed

Pemberley. "Everybody must be in their gardens this evening, guarding their snowmen."

They approached the bar.

"Did you notice anyone come in here just now?" Churchill asked the barmaid.

"Only yourselves."

"Before us, I mean. Did someone just rush inside this pub? Out of breath, as if they'd been running?"

The barmaid shook her head. "No. I haven't seen anyone come in for about fifteen minutes."

"Are you sure?"

"Very sure."

"The barmaid must be right, Mrs Churchill," said Pemberley. "If anyone had come in just before us they would have left little heaps of snow and wet footprints on the floorboards, just as we have. But the floor looked reasonably dry when we stepped in here."

"You're not wrong, Pembers. A pub floor is never a pretty sight, but there's no evidence of anyone having stepped inside just ahead of us." She glanced around at the drinkers' faces, trying to deduce whether anyone looked puffed out. "Everybody in here seems well-ensconced. I'm afraid we've lost the smasher again."

Chapter 27

CHRISTMAS EVE DAWNED, and the villagers gathered in Compton Poppleford marketplace to hear who would be crowned the winner of the Compton Poppleford Christmas Snowman Competition. A small stage had been erected next to the statue of deceased dignitary Sir Morris Buckle-Duffington. Someone, obviously in a festive mood, had placed a red hat with a white pompom on his head.

"I wonder how many snowman casualties there were last night," Churchill said to Pemberley as they stood among the throng.

"There can't have been many. Judging by how tired they look, most people here have been up all night. Mrs Harris can't stop yawning."

"I know the feeling. Isn't it disappointing, Pembers, not to have solved either of our cases in time for Christmas? There must be something we can do."

"At least we can rule Miss Broadspoon out as the snowman smasher."

"Very true. But that's not enough progress, is it? There was something Miss Broadspoon mentioned yesterday that interested me, though…" Churchill glanced around at the crowd.

"What was that?"

"Just something about Mrs Grainger."

"The headteacher who beat her pupils?"

"And apparently ran off with Mr Marrowpip."

Churchill spotted two girls aged about twelve or thirteen. Standing close to them was a woman in a fur-trimmed coat, whom she assumed to be their mother. She stepped over to her. "Good morning. I hope you don't mind me bothering you. My name is Mrs Annabel Churchill and I'm a private detective."

The lady looked her up and down. "Are you indeed? How marvellous for someone of your age to be doing such a job."

"Thank you… I think. I'd like to find out a little more about Mrs Grainger. I believe she was the headmistress at the village school. Perhaps your daughters attended while she was there?"

"They're not my daughters."

"Oh, I'm terribly sorry."

"One is my niece and the other is her friend. And yes, they do attend the village school."

"Do you mind if I speak to them about Mrs Grainger for a moment?"

The woman called over to the girls, who politely presented themselves to Churchill.

"I understand you attended the local school while Mrs Grainger was headmistress. Is that right?" she asked.

The girls nodded.

"What can you tell me about Mrs Grainger's sudden departure?"

They both shrugged.

"She just left," said one. She wore a blue hat.

"Yes, I realise that. But do you know why?"

The other girl, who wore a red hat, scratched her chin. "My mother said there was something in the newspaper about her."

"Do you recall what that was?"

"Someone said she hit someone."

"Interesting. Do you happen to know who she hit?"

"No," the girl in the blue hat replied.

"Did you know anyone who claimed to have been hit by Mrs Grainger?"

"No," said the girl in the red hat.

"Did you ever witness her hitting anyone?"

"No."

"Did she ever hit you?"

"No!" replied the girl in the blue hat. "She was nice."

"Mrs Grainger was a nice headmistress?"

Both girls nodded.

"She was *really* nice," said the girl in the red hat. "I was sad when she left, because then we got Mr Bockum."

"He smells," added the girl in the blue hat.

"I see. Thank you, girls. You've been very helpful."

"Stand to attention for Mayor Nettlehorn!" came a voice from the direction of the stage.

A small, wizened man, who appeared to be weighed down by the heavy gold chain around his neck, clambered onto the stage and wafted a weak wave in the general direction of the crowd.

"Thank you to everyone who entered the Compton Poppleford Christmas Snowman Competition," he began, his voice slow and dreary. "Despite some rather unpleasant acts of sabotage over the past few days, I'm pleased to say that we had a good number of entrants in the end. Even when one of the snowmen was smashed overnight, it was swiftly rebuilt just in time for the judges to make their rounds this morning. As you know, one of those judges was Inspector Mappin. I'd like to invite him onto the stage now to announce the winner."

There was a ripple of applause as Inspector Mappin joined the mayor with a proud expression on his face. He doffed his hat in appreciation.

"I wonder whose snowman was smashed overnight, Pembers," Churchill muttered.

"It sounds as though whoever it was managed to salvage it."

Inspector Mappin cleared his throat, then began. "Without a doubt, it's been a tumultuous few days in Compton Poppleford. It's been rather tricky finding the time to judge the competition because I've also been concentrating my efforts on an extremely important murder investigation." A hush fell over the crowd. "However, I would like to commend the efforts of all who have been involved in the building and, where necessary, rebuilding of their snowmen. And I must say to the hooligan who had no qualms about running around the village at night-time knocking down the snowmen people had spent time constructing: we *will* find you. There's no need to ruin people's fun in such a spiteful manner, especially at Christmastime. Anyway, that's enough of the miserable talk. I shall now announce the winner."

"Hooray!" responded a voice from the crowd.

Inspector Mappin held out his hand to take an envelope from the mayor.

"Why are you opening an envelope when you already know who it is?" someone called out.

"Quiet, please," said the mayor. "Have some respect for the ceremony."

"The prize is ten pounds," said the inspector as he opened the envelope and pulled out a piece of card. "And the award for best snowman goes to..." He paused for dramatic effect. "Dr Sillifant!"

A ripple of applause travelled through the crowd, and several cheers went up as the doctor made his way through the crowd.

"Bravo!" Churchill called out.

Dr Sillifant climbed onto the stage, then bobbed and bowed appreciatively in response to the applause. Churchill grinned and clapped, thinking how handsome he looked in his dark suit and festive bow tie.

"Thank you, thank you," the doctor called out to the crowd. "You're too kind!"

The mayor presented the doctor with a shiny cup and a cheque. Then the three men posed for the newspaper photographer with wide grins on their faces.

"Well done, Dr Sillifant!" exclaimed Churchill, secretly hoping he would notice her.

"But why did his snowman never get knocked down?" asked Pemberley.

"That's all forgotten about now, Pembers. The important thing is that the best snowman won."

Dr Sillifant signalled for the applause to end, and everyone obligingly quietened down. "A few words, if I may," he said. "Thank you so much, Inspector Mappin, and Mayor Nettlehorn for this award. I really didn't expect my humble effort to win at all. To be honest with you, I didn't think Sir Dennis was a particularly good snowman compared with the many wonderful snowy creations I saw in the village. Nevertheless, the judges have made their decision and I'm exceptionally proud. I would like to invite you all to a little Christmas Eve drinks gathering this evening at Coldbone Hall to celebrate. You can share in my joy at receiving this award and together we can spread a little festive cheer."

Another round of applause erupted.

"Isn't he a lovely man, Pembers?" said Churchill, clapping her hands even more loudly than before. "He's always thinking of others, even in his hour of glory."

"Very thoughtful of him," replied Pemberley.

The speeches were over and the crowd was beginning to disperse.

"There's Mrs Thonnings," Churchill said to Pemberley. "Let's go and see if she's come round."

"I'm sure she won't have."

Churchill approached her offended friend. "A worthy winner, wouldn't you say, Mrs Thonnings?"

The haberdasher pursed her lips and turned her face away.

"Oh, no. You're not still ignoring me, are you? I didn't mean to offend you. It's just rather difficult to carry out our detective work when there are so many suspects to consider."

"Bernard shouldn't be among them," Mrs Thonnings retorted as she turned on her heel and walked away.

"That's a shame, isn't it, Pembers? She still doesn't want to speak to us. Let's go back to the office and have another look at our incident board. I've been having a few thoughts."

"About what?"

"I'm not exactly sure yet. They're still fluttering about the place and I need to catch them in my net. When I returned home in the early hours of this morning, I mulled over everything everyone's told us in the last week or so. I've decided I'd like to speak to Mr Marrowpip. It seems rather odd that no one has seen or heard anything of him since his wife passed away. It makes one wonder whether he's even heard about it."

"Mrs Thonnings said he went off to Dorchester. How are we going to find him there?"

"Let's look up his address in the telephone directory at the library. Then we can pay him a visit."

"On Christmas Eve?"

"I'm afraid so. But hopefully we'll be back in time for celebratory drinks at Coldbone Hall. Won't that be something to look forward to?"

Chapter 28

AFTER A LONG DAY IN DORCHESTER, Churchill, Pemberley and Oswald trudged through the snow from the railway station to Coldbone Hall.

"It's certainly been an interesting, if rather exhausting, excursion," said Churchill. "I can't wait to have a little drink with Dr Sillifant. With a bit of luck, he'll have baked a fresh batch of mince pies."

"I don't see what all the fuss is about," replied Pemberley.

"What fuss?"

"Why you like Dr Sillifant so much. I think he has a very high opinion of himself."

"One might argue that it's a justifiably high opinion."

"In what sense?"

"Because he's a doctor, Pembers! And perfectly charming with it, too. Anyway, it was fun discussing our theories about the case on the train just now, wasn't it? I think we've come up with some useful ideas. Perhaps we can share them with Inspector Mappin if he attends Dr Sillifant's party."

"I think we should. Perhaps everything can still be resolved in time for Christmas."

Dusk was falling as they approached the Tudor cottage. Lights glowed in the mullioned windows and the cup for Best Snowman had been proudly placed next to Sir Dennis.

"I do like a party on Christmas Eve, don't you, Pembers? Songs and wine, and merry-making a-plenty."

"I'm feeling rather tired, actually."

"A glass of something festive will see you right. Good tidings we bring, to you and your kin."

"We don't have to stay long, do we?"

"Just wait till you step inside, Pembers. You'll be seized with festive cheer, and all tiredness will immediately be forgotten."

As they stepped over the threshold into Coldbone Hall, however, the senior detectives sensed an air of discontent.

Mrs Higginbath and Mrs Craythorne were angrily shouting in the hallway, though Churchill struggled to establish whether they were agreeing or disagreeing with each other. Miss Broadspoon was crying in the front room, and Mrs Harris was desperately trying to comfort her. Inspector Mappin appeared flustered whilst being harangued by Mr Groggins.

"Goodness! There doesn't appear to be a lot of Christmas cheer here, does there, Pembers?"

"I sense a gloomy atmosphere. Perhaps we should just leave?"

"I'd like to find out what's happening."

Churchill caught sight of a fretful Mrs Thonnings, but deduced that her former friend probably wasn't in the mood to talk. Instead, she accosted Mr Pouch. "Perhaps you can tell us what's happening here, Mr Pouch?"

"I've found my scarf! The one with the brown, purple and green stripes."

"And that's what's upset everyone?"

"Mrs Higginbath has recovered her brooch and Inspector Mappin has found his helmet."

"That's wonderful news!"

Mrs Thonnings caught sight of Mr Pouch and yanked him away to prevent him from speaking to Churchill any further.

Undeterred, Churchill turned to Inspector Mappin. "You found your old helmet, Inspector?"

"I certainly have. And I'm furious about it!"

"Why's that?"

"Because it was in Dr Sillifant's hallway cupboard."

"Who put it in there?" Churchill considered her question for a moment, realising she already knew the answer. A cold, heavy weight shifted from her chest to her feet. She tried to find some way to deny it, but it was no use. It was clear to see how Sir Dennis had escaped the attentions of the snowman smasher now. "Oh dear," she said. "Did Dr Sillifant put your helmet in his hallway cupboard? Along with all the other missing items? Is he really the snowman smasher?"

"He certainly is!" replied the inspector. "Mrs Higginbath was looking for the privy and accidentally opened the door to the hallway cupboard instead, happening upon the stolen items. Dr Sillifant's over there in the corner now, dealing with an angry mob. And they've got it in for me, too, because I awarded him the prize for Best Snowman! And to think that I decided his snowman was the best in the village while he's the one who's been going about smashing up everybody else's snowmen all along! I've been taken for a fool!"

"So have I, Inspector," admitted Churchill. "I suppose

it was obvious, really. The facts were staring me in the face. But I refused to acknowledge them. I didn't want to believe that Dr Sillifant could have done something so horrible."

"Nor did I. But it looks like I'm going to have to make an arrest." His fingers stroked the handcuffs hanging from his belt. "I'm just not sure what I can arrest him for yet. Vandalism, perhaps. Trespass. Something like that. Given that it's Christmas Eve, I'll just give him a night in the cells and let him out early so he can celebrate Christmas Day. But crime doesn't stop at Christmas, does it?"

"No, I'm afraid it doesn't." Churchill glanced around the room to establish who else was present. "Before you do anything, Inspector, I've a theory about Mrs Marrowpip's murder that I'd like to share."

"Really? Let's hear it, then."

"I'd like to announce it publicly, seeing as everyone's here. It won't take long. Do you mind calming everyone down while I stand over there by the Christmas tree and attract their attention? One thing I will say, Inspector, is that you'll need to have your handcuffs ready."

Chapter 29

ONCE QUIET HAD DESCENDED, Churchill thanked everyone for giving her a few minutes of their time. "As you're all aware, my assistant, Miss Pemberley, and I have been involved in an extremely complicated investigation over the past few days."

"We already know who it is," called out Mr Groggins. "It was Dr Sillifant all along."

"I'm not talking about the serial snowman smasher," responded Churchill, glaring at the doctor, who was standing at the side of the room with Inspector Mappin guarding him. "I'm talking about the tragic death of Enid Marrowpip. She was poisoned by a portion of plum pudding a few days ago, and it's been rather difficult for us to work out who was responsible."

"It was Mrs Higginbath," said Miss Broadspoon. "And all because Enid reported her to Dorset Central Library."

Churchill held up a hand to silence her. "Please allow me to do the explaining, Miss Broadspoon."

"But I *didn't* poison her!" protested Mrs Higginbath.

"May I be allowed to speak?" asked Churchill. "Good.

Thank you. Now, Miss Broadspoon, you're quite right. Mrs Higginbath had a motive for poisoning Mrs Marrowpip, who claimed to have seen Mrs Higginbath pocketing library fines."

"Disgraceful!" exclaimed someone.

"When will I get my money back?" protested another.

"That's out of my jurisdiction," replied Churchill. "You'll have to take it up with Dorset Central Library, which is investigating the matter. However, please remember that Mrs Higginbath is innocent of all charges until firm evidence is uncovered. Everyone must keep a calm head about it."

"I shall prove my innocence!" declared Mrs Higginbath.

"I'm sure you will," Churchill replied. "The fact of the matter remains, however, that Mrs Higginbath bore a grudge against Mrs Marrowpip for reporting her."

"How could I have done?" queried Mrs Higginbath. "I didn't even know it was Enid who'd complained about me."

"So you claim, Mrs Higginbath. Anyhow, let's move on to Dr Sillifant."

Booing and jeers filled the room.

"I want to know who really won the snowman competition," someone protested. "He should be stripped of his title!"

"Another matter that is out of my jurisdiction," responded Churchill. "But for what it's worth, I agree with you. Someone else should be given the Best Snowman prize. I must say that I was as shocked as everyone else to discover that a man as charming and accomplished as Dr Sillifant could stoop so low as to run around smashing up other people's snowmen. He's clearly not the man we all thought he was. But is he a murderer?"

"No!" he protested. "I admit I got a bit carried away with knocking down those snowmen, but it was only because I wanted to win the competition so badly. And it worked!"

"Briefly," said Mr Groggins.

"I'm not perfect," responded Dr Sillifant, "and I have knocked down a lot of snowmen. But I must insist, yet again, that I am *not* a murderer."

"But you also had a powerful motive for murdering Mrs Marrowpip, didn't you, Doctor?" queried Churchill. "She made a complaint which had resulted in you being suspended from the Dorset Medical Council. And what's more, you were informed at the outset that Mrs Marrowpip was the one who had made the complaint."

"But the matter is closed and no action was taken against me," he replied.

"It was only closed because Mrs Marrowpip is dead," retorted Churchill. "Possibly at your hands. You must admit that her death was rather convenient for you, wasn't it?"

"Why did she make a complaint about him?" asked Mrs Harris.

"I don't have the full details of the case, but according to the clerk Miss Pemberley and I spoke to, Mrs Marrowpip was concerned that Dr Sillifant was displaying an unhealthy interest in the value of her home."

There were gasps from around the room.

"A fact that becomes more pertinent when you consider that this beautiful house Dr Sillifant lives in once belonged to a patient, who left it to him in her will."

"It was all above board!" protested the doctor. He turned to Inspector Mappin. "You can check it over as much as you like, Inspector, but everything was done properly. This house was a genuine gift from a devoted patient."

"But it seems Mrs Marrowpip wasn't quite as devoted was she, Doctor?" said Churchill. "So perturbed was she by your inquiries about her home that she informed the Dorset Medical Council. I wonder if you had been putting pressure on her to change her will."

"No! When I asked about her home, I was merely making polite conversation. She lived in an extremely interesting property and I like old properties, as you know. That doesn't mean I wanted to inherit it when she died. Why would I need two houses? What good would two houses be to me?"

"You must have harboured some resentment towards Mrs Marrowpip when you discovered she had complained about you, and that you had been suspended from your job as a result."

"Yes, but I bore her no ill will. You witnessed that yourself at the Christmas dinner, didn't you, Mrs Churchill? I was perfectly polite and nice to her, and gave her immediate medical attention when she became unwell. Unfortunately, there was nothing I could do to save the poor lady; and that's a sadness I will live with for the rest of my days. However, given the high dose of cyanide she had consumed, nobody on this earth would have been able to save her."

"So, did he do it or not?" asked Mrs Higginbath.

"Let me continue," replied Churchill. "I must now move on to Bernard Pouch."

"Oh, here we go," protested Mrs Thonnings. "And to think that I once considered you a friend, Mrs Churchill!"

Churchill took a deep breath and continued. "Many of you will know that Mr Pouch ran a hardware store on Dogwood Street near the railway station, and that it wasn't a success. You will also know Mrs Marrowpip ran a very successful hardware store on the high street. At the fatal

Christmas dinner, Mr Pouch explained that he'd regrettably had to close his shop because it wasn't making enough money."

"I didn't even know there was a hardware store on Dogwood Street," someone called out.

"Well, there you go," replied Churchill. "That seems to have been the fundamental problem. Then, just four days after Mrs Marrowpip's death, my assistant Miss Pemberley and I became aware that Mr Pouch was running the hardware store on the high street. Now, this was quite understandable, given that his own store had closed and Mrs Marrowpip's death meant that there would have been no hardware stores open in Compton Poppleford had he not taken it on. It made sense, therefore, that Mr Pouch decided to speak to the landlord of the hardware store and arrange that he would take over the running of it. However, it's also quite possible that Mr Pouch engineered this opportunity for his own benefit. How convenient to find oneself running a successful hardware store when one's own has just floundered."

"No!" wailed Mrs Thonnings. "Bernard would never do such a thing!"

"She's right!" Mr Pouch firmly interjected. "I stepped in to run the hardware store on the high street so that I could continue to deliver an important service to the good people of Compton Poppleford. I was the only other person in the village with the expertise to run it."

"Make of that what you will," said Churchill, addressing the rest of the party guests. "Finally, I must turn to another attendee of that doomed Christmas dinner. That individual is Marigold Broadspoon."

Everybody turned to stare at the myopic lady with the large nose.

She rubbed at her forehead. "What have I got to do with anything?"

"Mrs Marrowpip was once a good friend of yours, wasn't she, Miss Broadspoon?"

"She was once a good friend of most people in Compton Poppleford," the lady retorted, "but she always had to ruin things. She liked to tell tales. We talked about that, didn't we, Mrs Churchill? She told tales on Mrs Higginbath and on Dr Sillifant."

"And she threatened to tell tales on you, too, didn't she?" probed Churchill.

"She did. But I would prefer not to disclose the nature of those tales."

"And quite right, too, because the tales refer to a rather personal matter, don't they, Miss Broadspoon? Something that need never become public knowledge. And to save your blushes, I shall agree not to reveal it to everyone gathered here now."

"Tell us!" Mr Groggins called out.

"That's quite enough," commented Churchill.

"Mrs Marrowpip was nasty," said one of the guests. "I'm not surprised someone poisoned her."

"It won't do to speak ill of the dead," said Churchill. "Especially not at Christmastime. While I realise she wasn't perfect, it's certainly not fair to suggest that she should have been murdered for her petty actions."

"Who's the poisoner, then?" Mrs Harris called out. "Was it Miss Broadspoon?"

"I think it was Dr Sillifant," said Mrs Thonnings.

"Quiet, please," said Churchill. "The sooner you stop speculating, the sooner I can tell you what I discovered shortly after the winner of the Compton Poppleford Christmas Snowman Competition was announced today."

A round of booing interrupted her as people jeered at Dr Sillifant once again.

"Quiet!" she shouted. "Thank you. Now, after that event, Miss Pemberley and I took a little trip on the branch line to Dorchester. And once we arrived there, we paid a visit to Mr Marrowpip."

Chapter 30

"I REMEMBER MR MARROWPIP," someone piped up. "How is he these days?"

"I'm not surprised he wanted to move away," commented another guest. "Fancy being married to Mrs Marrowpip!"

"Mr Marrowpip left this village five years ago," said Churchill, ignoring their interruptions, "to pursue an affair with Mrs Grainger, the local headmistress."

"The lady who beat small children?"

"Can you please stop interrupting?" said Churchill. "My throat's feeling rather dry and I could really do with a large brandy. Just let me finish what I need to say. So, my assistant and I had a chat with Mr Marrowpip, and we also had a chat with the new Mrs Marrowpip, the lady formerly known as Mrs Grainger. They both divorced their spouses and are happily married. Of course, there's no denying that Enid Marrowpip was extremely upset when her husband left her. And who wouldn't be? I'm sure it's not a pleasant situation to be in. Mr Marrowpip and the new Mrs Marrowpip have many regrets about their past conduct. But let me add that the former Mrs Grainger had left this village under a cloud."

"Because she beat up tiny children," someone said.

"If you believe what the *Compton Poppleford Gazette* reported, you might say that," said Churchill. "But we all know the saying, don't we? Never believe anything you read in the newspaper."

"Oh, come on, Mrs Churchill," greasy-haired Smithy Miggins, the local news reporter, piped up. "That's not fair!"

"I'm delighted you're here, Mr Miggins," replied Churchill. "Perhaps you're able to recall the article your newspaper printed, which claimed that Maggie Grainger had hit her pupils?"

He wiped his nose with the back of his hand. "Yeah, I remember that."

"And who was your source?"

"We've had this sort of conversation many times before, Mrs Churchill. A reporter never reveals his sources."

"Understandable. Tell us how the tip-off came in, then. Was it a phone call? A visit? Or a letter, perhaps?"

"It was a letter," he said. "That's all I'm prepared to say."

"Do you know who wrote the letter?"

"It was anonymous."

"Even so, did you have any suspicions about who'd written it?"

"I might have done."

"And what were those suspicions?"

Smithy Miggins scratched at the stubble on his chin and shifted his weight from one foot to the other while everyone in the room watched him. "Oh, all right, then. I had my suspicions because the letter contained such a strong criticism of Mrs Grainger that it sounded like a personal vendetta to me. Having heard the rumour that Mrs Grainger was having a fling with Mr Marrowpip, I wondered about the source of the letter and decided to do a little investigation work of my own. I took the letter in to Mrs Marrowpip's hardware store and observed the prices written on the labels. I discovered that the handwriting in the letter bore a strong resemblance to the handwriting on the labels. I'm not saying it was definitely Mrs Marrowpip who wrote the letter, but that was my suspicion at the time."

"Did you ask her about it?"

"No, I didn't. The writer of that letter clearly wished to remain anonymous."

"Very well. But if Mrs Marrowpip was the author of that letter, one could argue that her actions were driven by spite rather than any factual basis?"

"Yeah, I suppose you could argue that."

"Which begs the question, Mr Miggins, why your newspaper went ahead and published the letter."

"We published it because it was a good story, wasn't it? We shifted a lot of copies that day."

"Then you admit that you published that letter with no regard whatsoever for Mrs Grainger and her job?"

"That's right. That's how the newspaper industry works, Mrs Churchill."

"Some newspapers, perhaps. I've met journalists who are far more rigorous about their procedures. Did you not approach Mrs Grainger for any comment?"

"There was no point. She would only have denied it, anyway. I didn't expect her to move away because of it. That was a bit much."

"You made some very unpleasant accusations against her, didn't you, Mr Miggins?"

"It wasn't me who made them, Mrs Churchill. I was merely repeating them."

"To such a wide audience that the poor woman had no option but to leave."

"Perhaps she shouldn't have been having an affair with Mr Marrowpip, then none of that would have happened."

"You now consider yourself a moral judge, do you, Mr Miggins? You appear to have exacted a punishment on someone whose actions you deemed unreasonable."

"Now you put it like that, Mrs Churchill, I suppose I did. Look, it was five years ago, and I'm not proud of what I did. It surprised me when she left the village, but I can't change any of that now."

"Perhaps your newspaper could print an apology explaining that a mistake was made?"

"Yeah, we could do."

"I bet it'll be in tiny print at the bottom of the last page," said Inspector Mappin.

"But how did Mrs Grainger murder Mrs Marrowpip?" asked Mrs Higginbath. "She wasn't even at the Christmas dinner."

"How very observant of you, Mrs Higginbath," replied Churchill. "I'll tell you who *was* at that Christmas dinner, though. Mrs Grainger's brother."

"Who's her brother?"

"Mr Bernard Pouch."

"Bernard is Mrs Grainger's brother?" queried Mrs Thonnings. "I don't think I knew that. Wait a minute…"

Churchill watched the haberdasher's face change as she realised what this meant.

"No! He didn't do it!" she exclaimed. "I've already told you that, Mrs Churchill, Bernard would never do such a thing!" she grabbed hold of his arm. "He wouldn't hurt a fly!"

"If it were buzzing around my jam sandwich, I probably would hurt a fly, to be quite honest with you," said Mr Pouch. "You think I murdered Mrs Marrowpip because she drove my sister out of town, Mrs Churchill?"

"Yes, Mr Pouch. I believe that's exactly what you did."

"How would I have done that?"

"I believe that while those portions of plum pudding were being chaotically shifted around the table, you made the most of the confusion and dropped the poison into Mrs Marrowpip's pudding. You'd probably been waiting for an opportunity like that for a long time, and it finally came."

"Did you do it, Bernard?" wailed Mrs Thonnings. "Did you poison Enid?"

"I didn't think she'd actually die! I only wanted her to be a bit poorly over Christmas. I didn't realise how potent such a small amount of cyanide would be. She should never have behaved that way towards my sister. She had no idea how upset Maggie was to be forced out of the village and lose her livelihood." He turned to face Smithy Miggins. "I've a good mind to poison you, too! You've got no business repeating other people's lies. You ruined her life. You newspaper people ruin everything."

"I refuse to believe it!" cried Mrs Thonnings. "I just can't believe it! That explains why you wanted me to invite Enid, Bernard! I didn't want to invite her. She'd been nasty to everyone, going around telling tales, yet you talked me round and made me feel sorry for her. And now I understand why!"

"Mr Pouch insisted on Mrs Marrowpip being invited, did he, Mrs Thonnings?" asked Churchill. "It would have been helpful if you'd told us that sooner."

"If I had, you'd have accused him of murdering her. I didn't want to believe he was capable of such a thing."

"Very good, Mrs Churchill," said Inspector Mappin.

"But everyone seems rather surprised to learn that Mrs Grainger was Mr Pouch's sister. How did you work that out?"

"I recalled a comment he'd made at the Christmas dinner. Upon finding a piece of chalk in his Christmas cracker, he suggested that he would give it to his sister. Wondering what use his sister could possibly have for it, I privately deduced that she was in the teaching profession. When I later learned that Mr Marrowpip had run off with a teacher, Mrs Grainger became a person of interest to me."

"Very good Mrs Churchill." Inspector Mappin sauntered over to Mr Pouch. "Looks like I need to get the handcuffs on you, Bernard. Unfortunately, I've only got one set with me." He fastened them around Mr Pouch's wrists, then turned to Dr Sillifant. "That means you'll need to be on your best behaviour now, Joseph. No trying to run away while I escort you both down to the station."

Chapter 31

"I CAN SCARCELY BELIEVE IT," said Mrs Thonnings. She sat slumped in a chair in Churchill and Pemberley's office. "Bernard and I were planning to have such a lovely Christmas together, and now he's been arrested for murdering Enid. Under my own roof! I'm sorry I was so sulky with you, Mrs Churchill. I really didn't want to believe that someone I cared so deeply about could do something so awful."

"Perfectly understandable," replied Churchill, mindful of her recent infatuation with the snowman smasher Dr Sillifant. "I'm sorry you're not having a very merry Christmas."

"I had no idea he was a murderer!"

"Well, if he's to be believed, he didn't actually want to murder Enid. He just wanted to make her a bit unwell."

"And who can blame him?" said Pemberley. "She made life miserable for everyone just because a wrong had been committed against her."

"She won't be the first and she won't be the last," said

Churchill. "Now then, it's getting late and it's Christmas Eve. Father Christmas will be out delivering his gifts soon, and I think we all need to start feeling a little more festive. What do you have planned for Christmas, Miss Pemberley?"

"I haven't really thought about it yet."

"Even this late on Christmas Eve?"

"I suppose I was just looking forward to a quiet Christmas with Oswald."

They all looked at the little dog, who was happily warming himself beside the fire.

"He looks quite adorable in that little bow tie," said Mrs Thonnings. "Who does he remind me of? That's right, Dr Sillifant."

"Yikes!" proclaimed Pemberley. "I'll take it off him right away. None of us needs to be reminded of him. Least of all Mrs Churchill."

"No, leave it, Miss Pemberley," Churchill said. "Mrs Thonnings is right; Oswald does look adorable in his bow tie, and he doesn't remind me of Dr Sillifant one bit. In fact, I'd completely forgotten about that odious man. Who were we talking about again?"

"Dr—"

"It's all right." Churchill held up a hand. "I don't need reminding. Perhaps you and Oswald would like to join me at my cottage for Christmas lunch tomorrow, Pembers?"

"Yes, Oswald and I would like that very much."

"And you, Mrs Thonnings?"

"Well, now that Bernard's been arrested I don't have anyone else to spend Christmas with. So that would be lovely, Mrs Churchill. Thank you."

"I'll bring round some mince pies," said Pemberley.

"That would be much appreciated."

"I've got another plum pudding in the larder," said the haberdasher. "Shall I bring that?"

"No thank you, Mrs Thonnings! Just bring yourself. That will be more than enough."

The End

Thank you

Thank you for reading *Disaster at the Christmas Dinner*, I really hope you enjoyed it!

Would you like to know when I release new books? Here are some ways to stay updated:

- Join my mailing list and receive the short story *A Troublesome Case*: emilyorgan.com/a-troublesome-case
- Like my Facebook page: facebook.com/emilyorganwriter
- Follow me on Goodreads: goodreads.com/emily_organ
- Follow me on BookBub: bookbub.com/authors/emily-organ
- View my other books here: emilyorgan.com

And if you have a moment, I would be very grateful if you would leave a quick review of *Disaster at the Christmas Dinner* online. Honest reviews of my books help other readers discover them too!

Get a free short mystery

~

Want more of Churchill & Pemberley? Get a copy of my free short mystery *A Troublesome Case* and sit down to enjoy a thirty minute read.

Churchill and Pemberley are on the train home from a shopping trip when they're caught up with a theft from a suitcase. Inspector Mappin accuses them of stealing the valuables, but in an unusual twist of fate the elderly sleuths are forced to come to his aid!

Visit my website to claim your FREE copy:
emilyorgan.com/a-troublesome-case
Or scan this code:

Get a free short mystery

The Augusta Peel Series

Meet Augusta Peel, an amateur sleuth with a mysterious past.

She's a middle-aged book repairer who chaperones young ladies and minds other people's pets in her spare time. But there's more to Augusta than meets the eye.

Detective Inspector Fisher of Scotland Yard was well acquainted with Augusta during the war. In 1920s London, no one wishes to discuss those times but he decides Augusta can be relied upon when a tricky murder case comes his way.

Death in Soho is a 1920s cozy mystery set in London in 1921. Featuring actual and fictional locations, the story takes place in colourful Soho and bookish Bloomsbury. A read for fans of page-turning, light mysteries with historical detail!

Find out more here: emilyorgan.com/augusta-peel

The Penny Green Series

Also by Emily Organ. Escape to 1880s London! A page-turning historical mystery series.

As one of the first female reporters on 1880s Fleet Street, plucky Penny Green has her work cut out. Whether it's investigating the mysterious death of a friend or reporting on a serial killer in the slums, Penny must rely on her wits and determination to discover the truth.

Fortunately she can rely on the help of Inspector James Blakely of Scotland Yard, but will their relationship remain professional?

Find out more here: emilyorgan.com/penny-green-victorian-mystery-series

Milton Keynes UK
Ingram Content Group UK Ltd.
UKHW011847060923
428171UK00004B/167